SADIE'S ABSENT BEAU

Sadie's Story #2

BRENDA MAXFIELD

Tica House
Publishing

Sweet Romance that Delights and Enchants!

Personal Word from the Author

Dearest Readers,

Thank you so much for choosing one of my books. I am proud to be a part of the team of writers at Tica House Publishing who work joyfully to bring you stories of hope, faith, courage, and love. Your kind words and loving readership are deeply appreciated.

I would like to personally invite you to sign up for updates and to become part of our **Exclusive Reader Club**—it's completely Free to join! We'd love to welcome you!

Much love,

Brenda Maxfield

Chapter One

Now faith is the substance of things hoped for, the evidence of things not seen.

— HEBREWS 11:1 KJV

Daniel Jantzi shifted in his bus seat. He tried to interest himself in the scenery flashing past the window, but he couldn't do it. He'd left Hollybrook feeling confident that all was well between him and his girlfriend, Sadie Sutter. Now, he wasn't so sure.

He was expecting a lot from her; it was true. But she'd been understanding when he'd told her his father's debt was much greater than he'd thought, and therefore he'd have to stay up north working in the factories for a long time. She'd also been understanding when he told her they'd have to put off their engagement—secret though it would be.

She'd been right happy when he told her he'd take instruction to join church—which of course, he should have done the year before. Or even the year before that.

Why hadn't he anyway? His *rumspringa* was over—in truth, he'd hardly had it at all. His father needed his continual help on the farm. Daniel blew out his breath in frustration. His father had managed to plunge their family deeply into debt—even with the help of him and his brothers on the farm. So, Daniel ignoring and basically skipping his *rumspringa* had made no difference at all.

Without joining church, he and Sadie couldn't be wed. Sadie had joined church two years ago when he should have. Well, regrets wouldn't do him any good now. The only thing for it was to join church this coming fall and take care of the situation.

But he and Sadie still wouldn't be able to wed. Not with him up north working in the factories and her down in Hollybrook where they both belonged. Not for the first time, Daniel had to force down his resentment toward his father.

"You going to Render's Bend?" the stocky man sitting beside him in the bus asked.

"*Jah*," Daniel answered.

"You one of them Amish who works in the factories up

there?" The man puckered out his lips as if smacking a lollipop.

"*Jah*," Daniel said again—politely enough; although, he had no longing to continue a conversation with the man.

"Yeah, there seems to be lots of your kind up there. I always thought you Amish only built tables and farmed." The man guffawed and wiped a drip of spittle from his lip. "Guess I was wrong about that."

"Guess so," Daniel said.

"You ain't taking offense at my talk, is you?" the man continued.

"*Nee*. None at all," Daniel said, forcing a smile. The man seemed content enough with his answer, so Daniel turned back to stare out the window.

He simply couldn't shake his worry about Sadie. She'd promised to wait for him... But then there was that other matter he'd tried his best to ignore. Sadie and Aaron Mullet. When Daniel's brother had told him he'd seen Sadie and Aaron riding out together, Daniel thought for sure Abe had been mistaken. Sadie wouldn't do that. She was good and loyal and sweet.

She wouldn't step out on him. But then, what was she doing in a buggy with Aaron? Because his brother had seemed quite sure about it.

Daniel sighed and leaned his head against the glass. He should have asked Sadie, but when he'd tried to get the words out, he couldn't. Besides, she had been looking at him with such affection and eagerness, he hadn't wanted to spoil it. But now, he wished he had.

Just a simple question, and then he would have her answer and he could relax. It had to have been an innocent ride. Or extenuating circumstances. Or something.

More regrets. He shuddered. He needed to get himself under control. He needed to put his thoughts on God and His goodness.

He needed to, but he just couldn't.

Sadie grinned at herself in the tiny mirror above the bathroom sink. She leaned closer and peered into her eyes. She saw a glow there, a look of happiness. She could hardly believe she'd been able to see Daniel that weekend. He hadn't said he was coming. Indeed, she hadn't expected to see him for another month or so. *Ach*, but it had been wonderful to be with him again, even if only for a short while.

She backed away from the mirror and pressed her hand to her hair, smoothing it into its tight bun at the nape of her neck. She needed to get her *kapp* on. Even though she was excited at seeing Daniel, she hadn't been pleased by his news. She didn't want to wait a year or two or even three to be married. Considering the amount of his father's debt, Daniel might have to work at the factories for a very long time.

Oh, they could write. But writing was a poor substitute for being together. She was more than willing to move north and live with him there if he had only asked. But he hadn't asked, and she certainly wouldn't voice it first—that would be highly unseemly.

Why didn't you ask me, Daniel? she thought for the hundredth time.

Without meaning to, her thoughts went to Aaron Mullet. Had she ridden out with him enough to satisfy her father? Anger still surged through her at her father's mandate that she marry Aaron. *Ach*, but what Amish girl's father demanded such things? And just because her father wanted help on the farm…?

She stood still, an idea coming to her. Why hadn't she thought of it before? She could get a job. Then she could pay for her father to get a farm hand. That would get him the help he needed. Yes, why hadn't she thought of it before?

In truth, she wasn't sure it would make a bit of difference. She was quite certain her father had enough money to hire help. Why he wouldn't do it, though, puzzled her. It more than puzzled her. It angered her and made her feel used.

She sucked in a breath. *Forgive me, Gott. I know my father has authority over me, and I must be obedient. Forgive me.*

But Sadie had no plans to be obedient in this matter. And then, Aaron Mullet himself had come up with a solution to their situation. They would ride out together a few times and then tell her father that they didn't suit. Her father could hardly *force* Aaron to marry her.

Sadie left the bathroom and went to her room to fetch her *kapp*. Once that was in place, she went downstairs to find her mother.

"Morning, daughter," Eugenia Sutter said, turning from the stove.

"Morning." Sadie went to the cupboard to take down the plates and glasses to set the table.

"I hope you slept well. Are Rose and the other girls up?"

"Rose was stirring when I left the room, but I don't know about Martha and Debbie."

Eugenia frowned and set down the spoon she was stirring the bubbling oatmeal with. "*Ach.* Those girls. I'll get them."

"*Mamm*, wait."

Eugenia stopped, her brow rising.

"I've been seeing Aaron—"

Eugenia relaxed. "And your *dat* and I are right happy about it."

Sadie sighed. "I don't... *We* don't want to court."

Her mother frowned. "What? Why not?"

"We've been riding and taking walks, and we don't want to court."

"You don't like him?"

Sadie swallowed. Did she lie now? Because the truth was, she did like Aaron. In truth, she liked him quite a lot. But that was beside the point. She was in love with Daniel. She wanted to *marry* Daniel.

"We don't get along..." Inwardly, she cringed at the untruth.

"Sadie," her mother said, her tone now moving to scolding, "you haven't given it a chance. It's because of that Daniel Jantzi, *ain't so?*"

Sadie bristled. "I told you and *Dat* from the beginning that Daniel was courting me. How did you expect this to work out with Aaron?"

Her tone had grown surly, and she bit her bottom lip.

Eugenia stared at her. "Daniel is going to be neck-deep in bailing his family out for how long...?" Her mother shook her head. "You don't need to be waiting forever to get married."

"He's helping his *dat*. That's what we do, *Mamm*. It's who we are. Haven't you taught me this over and over? I think Daniel is admirable." She squared her shoulders. Truth was, she wished Daniel didn't have to be so admirable in this case. She wished Daniel's father himself would step in and take care of the mess he'd made.

"Have you told your father this? About you and Aaron not suiting each other?" Eugenia asked.

"*Nee.*"

Her mother sighed. "I expect you'd better."

"I thought maybe... Well, maybe you and I could tell him together."

Eugenia's look pierced Sadie. "If you're thinking that will make it go down easier, you're mistaken."

Sadie bit her lip. In truth, she did hope that would make it go down easier.

"You'd better tell him this morning, daughter. And I expect you'd better be prepared for him to have something to say about it."

Sadie raised her chin. "Then maybe he'd better talk to Aaron. This ain't just one way."

Eugenia's brow furrowed, and she studied Sadie. "What did you do, girl? Did you purposefully make yourself unappealing? Because I can't rightly think of any reason why Aaron wouldn't want to court you."

"I... I..."

Eugenia shook her head in disgust. "What did you do?"

"I... I didn't do anything." Dear Lord, what if her mother discovered that she and Aaron had planned this? That, as a favor to her, Aaron had come up with this ruse to pretend that they simply weren't a match.

Eugenia's eyes narrowed further. "Deception is a sin. I hope you know that."

"I *do* know that," Sadie said, fighting the guilt that surged through her.

"Tell your father." Eugenia gave her a probing look. "He's out in the barn with the milker."

"Now? You think I should go out there now?"

"*Jah.* Now."

Chapter Two

Sadie sucked in a breath and obediently went through the washroom and out the side door. The sun wasn't quite up yet, though the sky to the east was rosy, with pink tendrils spreading out like a Japanese fan. She paused for a moment, taking it in. Then she closed her eyes and forced herself to ignore the red warning flags flapping in her mind and heart. She'd rarely if ever told her father an outright lie. It wasn't her way. Even when she knew the consequences would be dire, she would admit the truth.

But she couldn't admit the truth now. If she did, her father would never accept what she had to say. He wouldn't listen to her pleading. He had his heart set on Aaron Mullet, and once her father's heart was set on something, it was nigh to impossible to change his mind.

She opened her eyes and straightened her spine. She might as well get this over with.

She entered the barn. Her father had lit two lanterns as it was still hard to see in the morning shadows. He was sitting on a stool, milking the cow, his forehead leaning on the cow's flank. Sadie cleared her throat and her father jolted back, turning to look at her.

"*Ach*, Sadie. You startled me."

"Sorry, *Dat*."

"What are you doing out here? The milking's almost done, if your *mamm* is stewing about it."

"*Nee*, she ain't stewing."

"Then what are you needing? Chicken feed is over there, if that's what you're wanting." He gestured with his head, his hands continuing their rhythmic squeezing of the cow's teats.

"*Nee*, that ain't it either."

"Then what?"

She stepped closer until she could reach out and pat Gertie's brow. "I... I was wanting to talk to you about Aaron."

Moses smiled. "I know you've been stepping out with him, *ain't so?* I'm right glad, Sadie. You'll see that it will all work out for the best."

"Uh, that's the thing. Um... Well, Aaron and I aren't suited.

He doesn't want to..." She paused only for the briefest of seconds, prepared to continue her lie. And in that flash of a moment—in that split second, she saw doubt enter his expression. She saw his suspicion, his disbelief even before she continued. She swallowed. "He doesn't want to court me." She finally ended, wanting to turn on her heel and run. But she stood there, and a shaking starting low in her belly.

Her father let go of the cow. He stood and turned to face her squarely. "He don't want to court you? He seemed right pleased with the idea not so long ago. What happened?" His voice was low, but thick and solid.

"I... Well, *Dat*, sometimes people don't get on the way one would think."

He shook his head. "It ain't that, is it, daughter? It's that you don't *want* to get on with Aaron Mullet. Is this still about that Daniel Jantzi boy?" Before she could even respond, he went on, "I won't have it. I won't have your disobedience. This is for your own *gut*."

"*Nee, Dat*, it ain't. It's for your *gut*. You told me so." By the look on his face, she knew she'd gone too far. She involuntarily took a step back.

He stared at her, not moving. And then, his eyes narrowed. "I'll have a talk with Aaron."

"*Nee, Dat!*" she cried, horrified. Aaron had been so kind to her, so willing to make sure things were cut off between them.

She couldn't have her father badger him. Aaron had done enough.

"We came to an understanding, Aaron and me. I want to know what he's thinking. The boy—"

"*Nee, Dat.* Please." She felt like a fool. What other Amish girl in the whole world had to beg her father to give up his idea of an arranged marriage? Even after all these days, Sadie still couldn't believe she was in this position. It simply wasn't done. If she were braver, she'd go to the bishop and see what he thought. But she didn't dare.

She simply didn't dare.

Her father had sat back down on his stool and was milking Gertie again—the pinging sprays of milk hitting the sides of the metal pail. She waited, not sure what to do. Was the conversation over? Should she leave?

"Go on in and help your mother with breakfast," Moses finally said. He didn't look at her, and she didn't wait for another word. She whirled around and ran out of the barn and back to the house.

Sadie's mother gave her a questioning look when she burst into the kitchen. "I don't reckon that went well," Eugenia said.

Sadie grabbed a knife and began slicing the bread for toast. She was too angry to speak. Besides, this was her mother's fault, too, wasn't it? Her mother was going along with it. Not that Eugenia could have stopped her husband. But still, she could have taken Sadie's side in this, couldn't she?

No. Not really.

Sadie dropped the bread onto a broiler pan and went to the cook stove. She opened the oven door and slid the pan inside, turning the dial to broil. She stood there, staring at the oven elements through the glass door, watching them turn red hot.

Red hot. That's how she felt right then.

"He'll find someone else for you. Another young man," her mother said.

Sadie blew out her breath. "No one else is going to go along with such a scheme," Sadie declared. "I can't think why Aaron Mullet went along with it in the first place."

Sadie suddenly pictured her father going around to every eligible man in the district, begging them to court his daughter. Nausea swept through her at the thought. Before, she'd said she felt like a horse at auction, but now, she simply felt pathetic, unwanted, and deeply, deeply embarrassed.

Eugenia sniffed. "I know this ain't done. But your father needs help. And he got this idea in his head, and he won't let it go."

"I'm going to find work," Sadie said, determination filling her. "I'm going to find work and pay for farm help. That ought to satisfy him."

Eugenia put her hands on her hips. "Where are you going to find work?"

"I don't know, but I will. It's a far cry better than *Dat* begging boys to court me."

Eugenia reached out and touched Sadie's arm. "Can't you give Aaron a real chance? He's a *gut* man."

"I know he's a *gut* man. And *nee,* I can't. This isn't going to work out. I told you." But Sadie knew that it could have worked out. Aaron was willing, and he'd seemed interested in her. She couldn't deny that.

"Just try again, Sadie."

"I can ask at the restaurants in town. I can be a waitress."

Eugenia shook her head. "Your *dat* ain't going to let you work for the *Englisch*, nor the Mennonites. You know how he is."

Unfortunately, Sadie did know how he was.

"I'll make things. then I can knit and sew fine. I'll sell them and earn the money."

"Daughter, you ain't thinking straight. You can't make enough to hire a hand."

"*Jah*, I can. I'll show you." But she knew her mother was right. It would take her months to knit enough dishrags and scarves to earn the money to hire someone. She'd have to think of something else.

Her mother patted her shoulder. "Let's just relax a bit, shall we? I'm sure the *gut* Lord has a solution for all of this."

Sadie stared at her mother. A solution? The only solution her parents would approve of was if she got together with Aaron Mullet, and that was out of the question. She glanced at the bread under the broiler. It had already turned golden brown and was now inching its way toward being burned. She grabbed a hot pad and took the broiler pan out of the oven, plopping it on a wooden cutting board. She carefully picked up each piece of toast by its corner and turned them over on the pan.

As her mother dished up the oatmeal and flipped the thick fat slices of bacon in the sizzling grease in the skillet, Sadie put the broiler pan back into the oven.

This wasn't over. Not for her or for her parents or for Daniel.

But it had to be over for Aaron Mullet.

Chapter Three

Aaron heaved the sacks of chicken feed into the back of his pony cart. He grunted under the weight of the fifty-pound sack of flour his mother ordered and set it atop the feed. Then he climbed into his cart and was about to snap the reins and get underway, when he saw another pony cart enter the parking lot. His heart lurched. *Sadie.* He loosened his grip on the reins and sat still, waiting for her to draw near.

But she turned her pony, heading for the other side of the parking lot. Hadn't she seen him? Or was she trying to avoid him? He frowned and secured the reins again, jumping out of his cart. He strode to the far side of the lot.

"Hello, Sadie."

She looked at him, and he knew she was feigning surprise.

"Oh, Aaron. Hello."

He smiled and reached into her open cart, taking her reins and securing them for her. "Are you running errands today?"

She nodded, not meeting his gaze.

"Everything all right?" he asked. *Ach,* but Sadie was a beautiful girl. He longed to touch the strands of her hair, so smoothly tucked beneath her *kapp*. He imagined they were soft and silky. How long was her hair, anyway? He knew it would flow thick and wavy; in his mind, he could see the gentle curls plummeting down her back.

She looked at him then, her blue eyes guarded. "Everything's fine," she said, her sweet voice filling him.

"Sadie?" he probed.

"*Jah?*"

"It ain't fine. I can tell."

Her breath gushed out in a sigh. "*Nee.* It ain't fine."

He wanted to climb up into her pony cart with her. He wanted to put his arms around her and fix whatever it was that was bothering her. "Tell me," he said gently.

Her eyes widened, and he saw tears begin to form. "*Nee,*" she said. "I... Well, it's going to be fine. Nothing to fret about."

"But you're fretting. I can see it."

She shook her head, looking flustered. "I'm fine. Truly. How are you?"

"Sadie, won't you tell me what's bothering you? We're friends, *ain't so?*"

She gave him such a vulnerable look that it shook him to his core. He fisted his hands at his sides to keep himself from reaching out toward her.

"What is it?"

She sighed. "It's ... well, it's the same thing."

He stiffened. It had to be her parents trying to force her to forget about Daniel and to court him. Was he really that unappealing to her? Was it really such an offensive idea? Didn't she like him at all? His thoughts swarmed through his mind, filling him with frustration and yes, if he were truthful, hurt feelings. He wanted Sadie to like him.

Couldn't she like him more than Daniel? Or at least as much as Daniel?

What a fool. Of course, she wouldn't like him as much a Daniel. She and Daniel were courting—had been courting for some time. He forced himself to relax, forced his shoulders to lower.

"I see," he told her. "I'm sorry, Sadie. Do we need to go riding again?"

"My *dat* is threatening to talk with you about it."

Aaron stepped back at that, shocked. Was there no end to the lengths Moses Sutter would go to? What was really behind this? He'd thought it was simply an effort to secure a solid future for his daughter. And once Aaron had found out that it was Daniel courting Sadie, he understood Moses's concern. Daniel would be working to save his family's farm for a good long time to come. He would be in no position to offer a wife a secure home.

But now, Aaron wondered. If Moses was prepared to come to him again, there had to be more to it.

"I'm coming for you tonight," Aaron told Sadie. "I'll be there at seven-thirty. We can talk about this some more—away from prying eyes."

Sadie shook her head. "*Nee*. It's all right."

"It ain't all right, Sadie. I'll see you tonight." And without giving her a chance to turn him down again, he walked away, straight to his pony cart. He was determined to get to the bottom of this. There had to be more to it.

There had to be.

Kevin Sommer stood outside the factory in Render's Bend

where he knew Daniel worked. He heard a lot of noise from within, men hollering, and the hum of large machinery. He'd wanted to go right on in, but he was stopped at the door by a guard. Even after he explained that he was there for a friend, he wasn't allowed inside. Safety concerns, the guy said. Kevin snorted. He wasn't a child. He could take care of himself.

But he didn't argue with the man. He'd bide his time. The guard told him that Daniel's shift was due to be over soon, so he didn't have much longer to wait.

He walked over to the metal fencing that surrounded the parking lot and leaned against it. He couldn't stay in a sour mood for long. In truth, he'd been flying high since the television man, Gus Strider, had spoken with him. Imagine being offered so much money to live for a while in front of television cameras. It boggled Kevin's mind. He was going to earn money by being on a how about Amish youth, and he didn't have to do a thing but travel to a big city and explore the place.

Kevin had a suspicion that it would involve more than that, but he'd worry about that later. All he could see in his mind was that large number with all those zeros behind it. Kevin hadn't told his folks about the offer; he hadn't needed to. He was over eighteen years old, and the Gus fellow had assured him that it was all legal.

In truth, Kevin hadn't even told his folks that he was going by bus to Render's Bend to visit Daniel. They'd figure he was out somewhere when he didn't show up for supper that evening. He supposed it wasn't very thoughtful of him to just take off, but the mood had come over him and he'd bought a ticket and jumped on the bus without a second thought.

He glanced over at the huge double doors into the factory. Some men were trickling out, looked tired and worn. What was the matter with them? Personally, he would be overjoyed if he was doing something besides farming. Didn't they realize the blessing of being here, earning money and rubbing elbows with the *Englisch*? There was just no accounting for some people.

He watched the guys leaving, seeing some smiles here and there, until he finally saw Daniel. Daniel didn't look any too happy. He simply looked eager to be out of there. He was heading toward a large bike rack, crammed with bicycles.

"Daniel," Kevin called, waving.

Daniel stopped and turned toward him. An incredulous look passed over his face, and then he burst into a smile, hurrying over.

"Kevin! What in the world are you doing here?" he asked, slapping Kevin on the back.

"I'm here to see you."

Daniel shook his head, as if not believing Kevin was truly there. "Are you going to work at the factories, too?"

Kevin smiled. "*Nee.* I've got something way better than that."

Daniel gave him a dubious look. "What do you mean?"

"I'm fixing to tell you all about it. Do you have to go right home? I'm starving. Is there a restaurant around here?"

Daniel's brow furrowed in thought. "Well, there's a chicken place not too far from here. But you can come home with me. I know Vern and Chloe will welcome you."

"They your *aenti* and *onkel?*"

"*Jah.*"

"I don't want to bother them. How about I take you out for dinner, and then we'll go to your *onkel's* place?"

"I'd have to tell them. Otherwise, they'll worry."

Kevin thought of his mother who was likely worrying that very minute. "Fine. But then, I'm taking you to a restaurant."

He was itching to tell Daniel about the television offer, for Gus Strider had asked him to provide suggestions for other participants in the reality show. Kevin knew the news would be better received after Daniel had eaten and relaxed a bit. Kevin had learned that the hard way by rushing in too many times to speak to his father when he was tired and hungry.

"All right. It sure is nice to see you, Kevin. I'm missing my friends from Hollybrook." Daniel took his bike from amidst the clutter of other bikes, and they started walking out of the lot and down the street. "You want to get on the handlebars? We'll get there a lot quicker."

"Sounds *gut* to me," Kevin agreed and hopped on, once Daniel had steadied the bike.

Chapter Four

Within an hour, the two friends were sitting together in a local hamburger place—the chicken restaurant now being too far away. Daniel leaned back against the vinyl seat, enjoying himself and enjoying the juicy cheeseburger Kevin had bought for him.

"So, how long can you stay?" he asked Kevin.

"Just till tomorrow. Will your *aenti* put me up?"

"She said you could sleep on the sofa. So, *jah*. You're set. Wish you could stay longer than one night."

"It'll be enough."

"What do you mean?"

Kevin grinned at him, and Daniel grew wary. He knew that

grin. He knew when his friend had some ridiculous scheme up his sleeve.

"You gettin' full?" Kevin asked.

"Quit changing the subject."

"I can buy you another cheeseburger if you want."

"I'm fine. Once I finish these fries, I'll be stuffed." Daniel took a slurp of the chocolate milkshake Kevin had also bought.

"*Gut.* Then, down to business."

"Business?' Daniel was already shaking his head, even before Kevin explained just what business he was talking about.

"I got an offer for a new job."

Daniel's brow raised. "A new job? Doing what?"

Kevin's eyes gleamed. "Being on television."

Daniel stared blankly at his friend. He must not have heard right. "What did you say?"

"Being on television." Kevin laughed. "You should see your face right now."

"But you can't be serious. What's the job really?"

"Listen, I know it's odd, but it's true. This *Englisch* guy—name of Gus Strider—came to me and offered me a part in a new show on the television. I don't even have to do a thing. Just live my life. Only not in Hollybrook. Likely in New York or Seattle or somewhere. It could be for two seasons. That's what he calls them, seasons."

Daniel held up his hand. "Wait. What? What are you talking about?"

"It's this show about Amish youth in the city. It can't be hard at all. But the best part is how much they pay."

"You get paid to do nothing in a city?"

"That's right."

"But they would be taking your picture all the time. This ain't right, Kevin."

"I'm on *rumspringa*. I ain't joined the church yet, so I can't be disciplined or shunned by the church. Not really."

Daniel shifted in his seat. "But it ain't right, Kevin. Your folks would die of shame."

"This ain't about my folks," Kevin retorted, his voice raising. "This is about *me*. My life. My money."

Daniel stared at him. "What did your folks say about it then?"

"They don't know. And what will they say? I'm on *rumspringa*. They ain't going to say anything."

Daniel seriously doubted that, but he didn't say so. He was still in shock that Kevin would even consider doing this.

"How do you know the guy isn't lying to you?"

Kevin dug around in his bag and pulled out a wad of money which he dropped on the table. Daniel's eyes stretched wide.

"Where did you get that?"

"From Gus Strider. I told you. And he's already paid me some money. This ain't nothing." He leaned across the table. "I'm going to be rich, Daniel. *Rich*."

How could this be? Daniel blinked, trying to absorb it all. "So, you'd be in this show for two years and you'd be paid *gut* money for it."

When Kevin told him the amount, Daniel nearly jumped from his seat. "You *can't be serious*."

"I'm serious. You just got to sign these papers and agree to do what they ask. It ain't nothing bad, Daniel. I asked questions. I ain't stupid."

"I never said you were stupid."

"*Nee*. You didn't." Kevin took a deep breath. "Here's the best part. They want you, too, if you'll agree to it."

"*What?*"

"You heard me. Think about it. You ain't a member of church yet either. You could earn all that money so fast. You wouldn't even have to work in the factories here anymore."

Daniel's breath caught. He swallowed hard. "How do you know they want me. I ain't heard a thing about it."

"They asked if I knew anyone. I told them about you. So, here I am."

Daniel swallowed again. Could this possibly be true? What would Sadie say about it? What would his parents say? And the bishop? He'd be having his picture taken all day long. He'd be plastered across the *Englisch* television screens.

"We'd be wearing our Amish clothes?" he asked.

Kevin nodded. "*Jah.* They especially want that. Our hats, too."

Amish people on television? Daniel had never heard of such a thing—but then, why would he have heard? He didn't keep up with *Englisch* doings. But this couldn't be right. The whole thing didn't set well.

"You already agreed?"

"I signed the papers." Kevin shrugged his shoulders. "I'd be a right fool not to. They're offering me all this money and all this adventure, and all I had to do was agree. There are going to be Amish girls on the show, too. Gus told me. Maybe we can get some girls from Hollybrook to join us. How about Donna or Pamela or Sadie?"

"Sadie?" Daniel's voice broke. *Careful, careful, you'll give yourself away.* He blew out his breath. "I think those girls are already members of the church."

"*Ach*, you're right. Well then, how about Mary or, what's that girl's name... Susie. *Jah,* that's it. How about Susie?"

"You think Susie's folks would let her go? You're crazy, Kevin."

Kevin huffed out a breath. "*Nee.* I think you're the one who's crazy. This money would solve your family's problems, wouldn't it?"

Daniel stared at his friend. Kevin was right. Two years on the show would more than solve his family's problems. Truth be told, it would not only solve his family's problems, but it would likely set him and Sadie up.

But ... television?

"I see you thinking," Kevin said. "You know I'm right."

"You're right that the money would be welcome. And it would take away the debt, but I don't know. This doesn't feel right to me."

"What's not to be right?" Kevin said, his voice full of exasperation. "You think too much, Daniel. You always think too much. Let's do it. We'll have each other. How could we get into problems if we have each other? Come on. Do it with me."

Daniel was torn. He looked down at the remains of his meal and let his mind go. With that kind of money, he could marry Sadie soon. He groaned. *Nee,* he couldn't. How could he take instruction and join church if he was busy making a television show for the *Englisch?* It would put their wedding off for a solid two years. Maybe, he could just do one year. That would get his father out of debt for sure and for certain. And it would accomplish it a lot faster than this factory job. The way it was going right now—the last time he figured it out—he could be up here working in the factory for close to three years. *Three years.* Much longer than he'd originally thought. How could he expect Sadie to wait that long?

"Talk to your folks if you must," Kevin said. "They won't like it, you know. You should just sign the papers, then they'll have no choice but to let you go."

"You think your folks are going to be all right with this because you already signed the papers?"

"They got no choice, do they? I can't go back on a promise."

Daniel's throat tightened. The cheeseburger he'd just eaten felt like a rock in the bottom of his stomach. "They won't like it."

"*Nee.* They won't. But they can't do anything about it, can they?"

Daniel shook his head. He never did like the way Kevin got on with his folks. It was like there was a something always boiling under the surface. Daniel wanted peace with his own folks. He wanted his family to get along. How could he sign papers like that without their knowledge?

"Your *dat* would be grateful to you," Kevin said. "He already sent you up here, didn't he? How could he complain if you found a way to make the money more quick-like?"

Daniel swallowed hard. Maybe Kevin was right. Maybe his dad would be grateful.

"Come on, Daniel. Think of the fun we'd have. I mean ... what an adventure..."

Daniel's discomfort rose a notch. "If I ever agreed to do it, it wouldn't be because of the adventure," he said. "I don't need adventure. I want to pay off this debt and get back to Hollybrook."

Kevin studied him for a long moment. "Funny how we're such *gut* friends. We're total opposites."

Daniel smiled then. "That we are. Both *gut* friends and total opposites, I mean."

"Will you do it?"

Daniel had lived long enough to know not to ignore his gut. And his gut was screaming at him right then. "I don't think so..."

"*What?* You're not going to do it?" Kevin threw out his hands. "Are you crazy?"

"It doesn't feel right."

"Will you at least think about it?"

Daniel sighed. "I'll think about it."

"Truly?"

"Truly. I promise. I'll think about it."

"I still think your dad would be grateful."

Daniel knew his dad would like the money, but he was quite certain he wouldn't like or approve of the means.

"So I came up here for nothing?" Kevin asked.

Daniel laughed at that. "So, you don't really care about visiting me?"

Kevin laughed with him. "With you? *Ach,* why in the world would I want to visit with you?"

And they both chuckled.

Chapter Five

That night, Kevin slept on the front room davenport at Daniel's uncle's house. Daniel had offered him his bed in the laundry room, but Kevin turned him down. Daniel had left the laundry room door open, as he sometimes did, and he could hear Kevin's snoring. He gave a rueful smile in the dark and stared at the ceiling.

Kevin on television? Kevin making all that money? Daniel had a strong fear that once Kevin got that involved with the *Englisch*, he might never come back. Kevin didn't say as much, but he'd always been restless in Hollybrook. He'd always wanted to go just that bit further with everything. He tempted fate, Daniel thought. But he rarely got caught. Kevin had an uncanny sense about how far he could go without getting in trouble.

It was odd that they were such good friends, for Daniel wasn't the sort to step over the lines. In truth, he liked the lines. He had no problem with them. *Ach*, but he missed home. Missed Hollybrook.

Missed Sadie.

What was to become of their courtship? Surely, they could keep it going with letters. And he would have to make sure he went back often enough to see her. Would once every month be enough?

He closed his eyes and imagined her. It was easy to see her in his mind, for she was never far away from his thoughts. How he loved her. Hoe he wanted to make her his own.

Patience. Patience...

And then, unbidden, Aaron Mullet's image crowded into his mind. Daniel sucked in a huge breath. There was nothing going on with Aaron. Hadn't Sadie's behavior with Daniel proved that when he'd been home last? Sadie loved *him*, not Aaron. He was borrowing trouble by worrying about it. And if he kept on, he would drive himself crazy.

He stifled a laugh. Crazy. Maybe Kevin was right, and he *was* crazy, but not for the reasons Kevin thought. *Ach,* but he needed to get to sleep. The morning was going to come right fast, and he had to be at the factory bright and early.

Sadie did not want to go out and meet Aaron that evening. When the clock reached seven-twenty-five, she'd decided to ignore the whole thing, but then she panicked. Would Aaron come to the door and knock if she didn't show up? No. No. Certainly not.

But the problem was, she wasn't certain. Everything had gone upside down in her life, and she wasn't certain of anything anymore.

So, at seven-thirty, she put on her coat and slipped out of the house, hurrying across the yard to the road. She saw his buggy looming in the shadows as if it were twice its normal size. Goodness, but she needed to get ahold of herself.

The passenger door opened, and she got in.

Aaron smiled at her. "*Gut* evening, Sadie."

Was it a good evening? She highly doubted it. "Hello, Aaron."

Once she'd shut the door, he snapped the reins, and they were underway. Neither spoke until the buggy neared the edge of town. "Shall we walk at the park again? Or would you rather we just rode?"

She sighed. She'd rather be back home in her own room, writing a letter to Daniel. "It doesn't matter."

"Tell me what you prefer."

She frowned. He always wanted her opinion, and usually it

made her feel good. Important and respected. But right then, it only annoyed her.

"Let's walk," she finally said, knowing he wouldn't give up until she said one way or the other.

He pulled the buggy into the parking lot. She got out quickly, not wanting him to come around and open the door for her. If he did, it would seem more like a date, and this definitely was not a date. They started down the path side by side.

"You're angry with me," he said simply.

She didn't answer because, in truth, she was angry with him.

"You don't want to be here with me," he said. "And you don't want to talk about the situation. But I need to understand this. There has to be more, Sadie."

Sadie cringed. He was right; there was more, but that didn't mean she wanted to talk about it.

"I don't understand why your *dat* is so consumed with the idea of you marrying right away. Why does it matter? You're hardly an old *maidel*."

He was walking close to her—too close for her comfort. She tried scooting over a bit, but he scooted over right along with her.

"So, no laughter about the old *maidel* comment?" he continued. "*Ach*, but you really are angry with me."

"I'm not," she said, realizing now that it was her father she was angry with. Aaron was involved through no fault of his own.

"I think you are."

"I *am* angry," she said, shocked that she was admitting it out loud. Anger was considered a sin in her community, and certainly not something one would admit to freely.

"With me?"

"*Nee.* My *dat.*"

He nodded and was silent a moment before continuing. "I can see that."

She shrugged.

"What is the real reason he wants me to court you, Sadie. There has to be something more. It's like he's possessed with the idea or something. I mean, I know I'm a nice guy, but I hardly think I'm worthy of this kind of focus."

She looked at him then. Looked at his concerned expression, the look of affection in his eyes. He was wrong. He was worthy of this kind of focus, just not from her.

"My *dat* has always... Well, he's always been this way when he gets something in his head. I'm sorry, Aaron. I'm sorry about all this." She spread her hands in frustration. "It's embarrassing."

He grabbed her forearm and pulled her to a stop. His face was close to hers—so close that if it were earlier in the day, she could have seen the golden flecks in his brown eyes. Despite the park lights on the pathway, it was too dark to see them clearly, but she knew they were there just the same. Standing there with him, so still, in the nearly empty park, she felt his strength, felt his care for her, felt his curiosity.

"What is it, really?" he asked in a near whisper. "You are a beautiful girl, Sadie, and you will marry easily. I know... I know you have your heart set on Daniel, and if he has any sense at all—which I'm sure he does—he's working out a way to be with you this very minute."

Tears burned in Sadie's eyes. She hoped Daniel *was* working out a way for them, because she was afraid. It wasn't the first time she'd felt this fear, either. She tried to stuff it down, but she couldn't do it. If Daniel didn't come up with a solution soon . . .

Fear that things weren't going to work out between them tumbled through her. Something had to be done—of that she was certain.

She couldn't help with Daniel's family's debt, but she could help her father get a worker. And that was what she planned to do—at least that way, Aaron would be free of the mess. And she would be free of Aaron.

She flinched. What an odd way to put it. Free of Aaron.

Wasn't she already free of him? Just because they were there together right then didn't mean anything. Aaron was simply concerned for her, and likely sick and tired of being pulled into her problems. *Ach,* but what was her father thinking?

"I... I'm going to get a job," she blurted.

Aaron blinked. "What? I don't understand what that has to do with any of this." He visibly stiffened, and his eyes grew cold. "Is that what this is? If I marry you, then my folks new farm here will profit your father somehow? Through you?"

She sucked in her breath. "Your farm? *Nee,* that ain't it!"

"Then what is it?"

Sadie felt like a fool. What in the world was she doing there anyway? Why did she ride out with him that night? She should have just ignored him, which is what she'd wanted to do in the first place.

"Sadie, answer me." His eyes were so intent on hers that she felt uncovered, as if her *kapp* were off kilter and her hair were exposed. *Nee,* worse than that... As if her heart were laid bare for him to inspect.

"All right," she finally agreed. "My *dat* is getting on in years. He's getting tired of working the farm by himself. He has no sons. He thought that if you married me, he would have built-in help. You could work the farm with him."

She felt so ashamed that she couldn't look at him. She cast her eyes downward, wanting to be anywhere but there.

He reached out and touched her chin with his finger, raising it until she was forced to look into his eyes. She swallowed and fought the tears that threatened to fall. She hadn't been joking when she'd told her father she felt like a horse at auction. But as she met Aaron's gaze, something shifted. He wasn't looking at her as if she were on the auction block. He was looking at her with so much tenderness and understanding that her breath caught.

"*Ach,* Sadie. I'm so sorry," he murmured. His fingers were still on her chin, and she felt his touch as though it were burning through her.

She blinked and felt her tears begin to fall. He gently rubbed them away with his thumb.

"I get it now," he told her. "But in a way, it still makes no sense. Why doesn't he just hire help?"

"I don't know," she said. "I think he has the money. Maybe he just wants to keep it all in the family."

He nodded, not taking his eyes from her.

"I'm sorry," she murmured, her voice breaking.

"*Ach*, no reason for you to be sorry," he told her. "I'm just sorry you got caught in the middle."

"That's why I want to get a job. I'll pay for the help. Then you can forget about this whole disaster."

Aaron dropped his hand and turned away, looking into the distance for a moment. Sadie heard someone in the park hollering to another person and then a burst of loud laughter. At least two people were enjoying their walk in the park.

Aaron turned back to her. "I don't think I can forget this."

She frowned. "But why not? You can walk away. This whole thing was absurd in the first place."

"Maybe it was," he said slowly. "But now, I know you. We're friends. I want to help."

"But you can't. What can you possibly do?"

He smiled at her then, a mischievous smile, his lips curving up and his eyes now twinkling.

"Why, I can marry you, of course."

She blinked in surprise and for a moment, she thought he was serious. But looking at his grin, she realized he was teasing her.

She laughed. "Don't be silly."

The teasing expression on his face faltered for a minute, but then it was back. "It would solve your problem, wouldn't it? Except for Daniel, of course."

"Except for Daniel," she repeated softly.

He took her hand and started walking. Even though she loved the feeling of his fingers curled around hers, she pulled away from his grasp. He looked down at her but didn't say anything. They continued around the path, both of them silent once again.

After they'd walked a fair piece, she began to relax in his presence. Despite everything, he really was a comfortable person to be around.

"Well, at least now you know the whole truth of it."

"And you say your *dat* might talk to me again?"

"Not if I can help it."

He shook his head. "He really is single-minded, *ain't so?*"

She gave a rueful laugh. "That he is."

"I don't regret it."

She looked over at him. He gaze was straight ahead, not looking at her, and she saw his fine profile. The shadow from the brim of his hat couldn't hide the fine line of his nose and the strong set of his chin.

"You don't?" she asked.

"*Nee.*" He gazed at her then. "Not for a minute. If this hadn't happened, I wouldn't have gotten to know you."

She swallowed. This was becoming too intimate. She knew he

liked her, but there was something in his voice that had gone beyond mere liking. She took in a huge breath.

"Maybe we should head back," she said, coming to a stop.

He stopped, too. "If you think so," he said, and the two of them turned back toward the buggy.

Chapter Six

Daniel's day at the factory passed like molasses dribbling down the sides of a jar. Would his shift never end? Kevin would be gone, of course. He was to take the bus back to Hollybrook that morning. Daniel had nothing to look forward to at the end of the day. Oh, he'd enjoy playing with his cousins for a while, and his aunt would have a good supper on the table.

Once again, Daniel realized that Render's Bend wasn't his home. He didn't belong here. He belonged in Hollybrook with his family and friends. The only bright spot of the day would be writing to Sadie.

After supper that evening, Daniel excused himself to his room after only chatting with his young cousins for a few minutes.

He was eager to write Sadie. He lit the lantern that balanced on the wringer washer next to his bed and got right to it.

Dear Sadie,

How are you? I'm missing you so much. Would you believe that Kevin Sommer came to see me? I was right surprised to see him waiting for me outside the factory a day ago. But it was nice to see a friendly face. He's already gone, having left on the morning bus.

He had news. I don't know what you'll think of this, and in truth, I'm asking you to keep quiet about it since he hasn't told his folks yet, but he's going to be on a television program. I was more than shocked, truth be told. There is going to be a program about Amish people living in the city. They want young people, like us.

Kevin tells me that all he has to do is live in the city. I don't see how that will be much of a program. But Kevin is all for it. They're going to pay him a tidy sum.

The thing is, he wants me to do it, too. I said nee. What would the bishop think about this? Kevin says that since he's on his rumspringa, it is fine. It doesn't seem fine to me.

What do you think about it? I want to hear your thoughts. Do you think it's wrong?

Daniel paused. Why was he asking her opinion if he'd already told Kevin no? Was he entertaining thoughts about the possibility of it? He couldn't be. It wasn't right. No matter what Kevin said, it wasn't right. But oh, the money... He blew out his breath, disgusted with himself. Since when did he do things only for the money?

How is your family? How are your folks? I imagine the men are eager to get the seeds in the dirt. Still a bit early, though. Not much farming in the community here. Nearly all the Amish men work at the factory. There are a few who make furniture, but that's about it as far as I can tell.

I wish I could see you. I wish we were riding together in my dat's *buggy. Take care, Sadie.*

All my love,

Daniel.

Daniel folded the letter and tucked it into an envelope. He would address it and stamp it in the morning. Right then, he wanted to turn off his thoughts and his yearnings. He snuffed out the lantern, and even though it was an hour or two before his regular bedtime, he crawled under the cheerful quilt his aunt had made years before.

But Daniel didn't feel cheerful at all.

Kevin stood in the barn with his hands fisted at his sides. That couldn't have gone worse. He stared at the bridles hanging on the wall of the barn, his vision blurred with anger. Couldn't his folks understand the opportunity he'd been given? Couldn't they understand what this money would mean to his future?

He'd even offered to share it with his family, which was a common thing, but even so, his father was adamant.

"You will not do it," he'd said, his face reddening. "No son of mine is going to be caught dead on *Englisch* television."

"It's too late, *Dat*," Kevin had told him. "I signed the papers. I made my promise."

"You can unmake it then," his father snapped.

"It don't work that way. Gus Strider told me—"

"Gus Strider? What kind of name is that? You already taking up with the *Englisch,* and you haven't even left yet."

"I had to talk to him about it. He's the producer of the program. He's the one who told me all about it."

"Why didn't he talk to me. I'm your *father*."

"I'm over eighteen, *Dat*. He didn't need to talk to you."

His father had stormed out of the room then, but Kevin

knew it wasn't over. His dad would stew and fret and come back at him with more arguments. Kevin sighed. What had he expected? That his father and mother would send him off with their blessings? That would never be. So why was Kevin surprised now? Or angry? He'd known this was coming.

Still...

"Can't they trust me?" Kevin muttered, unable to curb his anger. "For once?"

But even as he questioned their trust, he knew he hadn't earned it. He'd been a thorn in their sides for most of his life —unlike his siblings who seemed to thrive under all the rules and obligations of the Amish way of life.

But not him. He'd challenged everything from the time he was a young boy. He couldn't seem to help himself. Nothing seemed fair. Nothing seemed fun. He had to make his own fun, sometimes at the cost of the rules.

Well, fine.

Leaving for the television show would be nothing to surprising then. Not really. He'd go, and he'd have an adventure, and he'd make more money than he'd ever seen in one place. He'd show his folks. He'd prove that it was a good idea. And then his mother could stop crying, and his father could stop hollering at him.

In truth, his father didn't exactly holler. When he was angry, his voice lowered. But it didn't matter. There was no mistaking the emotion there.

Kevin walked to the horse stalls and grabbed a pitchfork. He'd muck out the stalls. The activity would make him feel better.

Or so he hoped.

Chapter Seven

Sadie pressed Daniel's letter to her chest. "Can you finish the mopping?" she asked Rose. "I want to go read my letter."

"Go on," Rose said, taking the mop from where Sadie had dropped it in her excitement. "But you can do my share of the dishes tonight."

Sadie grinned at her sister. "I will." Then she turned and flew up the stairs to their bedroom. She sank onto the bed and ripped open the letter. She read it quickly, hearing Daniel's voice in her head as she read. When she got to the part about the television show, her reading slowed. What was this? She'd never heard of such a thing.

And Kevin had asked Daniel to participate? She breathed out in relief when she read that Daniel had turned Kevin down. She read that part again, and a sense of unease began to niggle at her. If Daniel was so set on saying no, why did he ask her opinion? It was almost as if he would reconsider if she didn't think it was so bad.

But she did think it was bad. How could Kevin have considered it—but in truth, she knew how. This sounded exactly something Kevin would jump at. Again, she wondered how he and Daniel were such good friends. And it sounded like being in the show was a for sure thing for Kevin.

The bishop was going to be right upset when he heard about this. And the deacons, too. Sadie thought of Deacon Elias and his harsh manner and ready judgement. If he had his way, Kevin would be disciplined. But then, like Daniel had pointed out, Kevin was on his *rumspringa*. As far as Sadie could recall, Kevin had been on his *rumspringa* for years.

Maybe this work with the television people would be the final straw, and Kevin wouldn't come back to the fold. Sadie sucked in a breath. Daniel wouldn't do it with him, would he? He said he wouldn't, but there was something about the way he had asked her opinion. Quickly, she grabbed her tablet and pen out of her nightstand and started writing.

Dear Daniel,

I got your letter about Kevin. I have to say that I was right surprised by what you told me. I can't even imagine such a program. And truth be told, I'm surprised that any Amish person would agree to it.

. . .

Sadie paused. For the money... That was why. Although, knowing Kevin, it would be for the excitement of it, too. Was Daniel tempted? How much money was involved?

Daniel needed money, and he needed it right away. Would he change his mind? A sick foreboding swept through her as she continued to write.

I'm glad you told Kevin nee. *I know you haven't joined church yet, but I don't think you consider yourself on* rumspringa *like Kevin does. I think this will break his* mamm's *heart when she finds out. I don't see how Kevin can keep it quiet—after all, he's going to have to leave Hollybrook to do it. I can't imagine anyone's folks being happy about their* kinner *participating in something with the* Englisch. *And on television! All those photos.*

I fear for Kevin. This can't be gut.

Sadie drew in a deep breath. Was that strong enough? She reread what she'd written. Yes. It seemed strong enough. Her opinion was clear. Daniel would have no doubt about her feelings. She tried to think of something newsy to tell him, something happy and interesting, but her brain couldn't seem to budge off the television program.

. . .

I hope you have a gut *week, Daniel. I'm thinking about you and praying for you.*

My love,

Sadie.

She folded the letter into an envelope and addressed it, and then she ran downstairs and found a stamp in the bureau in the front room. She passed by her sisters Debbie and Martha who were busy dusting.

"Where you running to?" Debbie asked her.

"Can we come?" Martha asked.

"I'm not going anywhere," she answered, passing them and pushing through the front door. She ran down the porch steps and headed across the yard with Daniel's letter clutched in her hand. She saw her father at the barn door, watching her. She slowed, but she could tell by his expression that he'd seen the letter.

"Sadie," he called her over.

Even though it was too late, she tried to hide it. But then something in her hardened, and she held the letter in plain sight.

"Who are you writing to?"

She squared her shoulders. "Daniel Jantzi." Despite her bravado, she was trembling inside.

Her father's eyes narrowed, and his lips tightened into a straight line. He stared at her for a long moment before asking, "Why?"

His question startled her. Wasn't it obvious why?

"B-because we're friends," she finally answered.

He took the letter from her, and she barely kept herself from snatching it out of his hands. He stared at Daniel's address.

"You been writing him all this time?"

She blinked but nodded.

His gaze flickered for a moment, and she saw sadness there behind his eyes. Expecting only anger from him, she was shaken.

"*Dat?*"

He licked his lips. "Knowing my feelings on this, you continue to write the boy?" His voice was low and filled with recrimination. She looked into his eyes for the sadness again but was only met with consternation. Maybe she'd been mistaken. Maybe he hadn't been sad at all.

"*Jah*," she answered him. She felt compelled to apologize, but in truth, she didn't feel sorry. Oh, in a way, she supposed she was sorry she'd disobeyed, but she *had* to write to Daniel. It was her father's doing that had created this entire mess. Parents weren't to interfere with their children's courting. It wasn't done.

And the fact that her father had done it still burned through Sadie's heart.

Her father tucked her letter to Daniel in his waistband. Sadie's chest heaved. Was he going to read it? She stared at the envelope, not believing what was happening.

"Will you give it back?" she asked, her voice faltering.

"Should I?" he questioned. "You've disobeyed me."

"You never told me not to write to Daniel."

He snorted. "I didn't think it was necessary. You know my wishes."

"Aaron doesn't want to marry me!" she cried.

Her father shook his head slowly. "That's where you're wrong, daughter. He wants to marry you."

She stepped back. "*Nee... Nee,* he doesn't. He told me so."

"Did he?"

She swallowed. No, Aaron hadn't said that right out, but it was understood between them. Had her father gone to Aaron again after all? Because Aaron would have told her the other night when they were talking about it. She pressed a hand to her mouth. Had Aaron betrayed her? What had he said?

What in the world *had he said?*

Her father was watching her and surprisingly, his expression softened. He pulled the letter from his waistband and handed it back to her. "I trust you not to mail this."

She reached out with a shaky hand. Nothing in her world made sense right then.

"I'm going to get a job," she said. "You're right, *Dat*. You need help on the farm. I'm going to get a job and then you can hire someone. There are plenty of boys who want work."

His brow raised. She was talking fast—way too fast, but she plunged ahead.

"You won't have to pay for it. I'll pay—" she broke off. Her father was glaring at her.

"You think this is only about getting me help?"

"You... You said it was, *Dat*. You're the one who tol—"

"That ain't all of it." His voice was harsh. "I know you're angry at me and your *mamm*. Do you think that pleases me? But I'm the head of this family. I do what I think is best, whether my daughters or my wife are in agreement. *Gott* has put me over this family, and I take that responsibility seriously."

"I-I know, *Dat*..." And she did know. She knew the way families were run. She knew how it was.

He sighed, and she saw his age then, saw it in the way his

shoulders slumped for a brief second before he straightened them again. "You can get a job if you must. In truth, it might be a *gut* idea—give you something to think on during the day. You'll have to check with your *mamm* and be sure she can do without your help. But you won't be using your wages to buy me help."

"So, it ain't the money," she said, although she had always doubted this was about a lack of money on her father's part.

"It's about you, daughter."

She stood in front of him, wondering what to say or do. She felt the letter to Daniel in her hand as though it were burning through her skin. She needed to mail it. Daniel needed to know her feelings about the television program. What if he decided... No. No. He wouldn't do that. He *wouldn't*. She flinched and realized her dad was staring at her.

"Aaron is willing to continue courting you."

"But *Dat*..." Her voice faded as confusion filled her. Aaron had agreed...? *Ach,* but this entire thing was completely out of hand. And what was the use? She was trapped, and she knew it. She stared at the letter in her hand and knew she couldn't mail it. Guilt clenched at her stomach. She should never have deceived her father in the first place. It was wrong. How could she please God if she continued with such rebellious behavior?

And she did want to please God. And she was a member of

church. She had promised to live by the *Ordnung*, promised to follow the Amish way of life.

Which included obeying her father.

But Aaron? How could he? She liked him—she truly did. But how could he betray her like this? Weren't they friends?

Without another word, she turned and walked slowly back to the house. When she entered the side door, she went through the kitchen and into the front room. The warming stove was burning low, emitting an even heat throughout the room. She knelt before it, opened the heavy metal door, and tossed the letter inside. She paused before shutting it again, watching the letter curl at the edges then catch on fire, burning her words from the page, leaving nothing but red-hot ash.

Chapter Eight

Daniel asked his aunt twice if there had been any mail for him. Both times, his aunt had told him no. The second time, she'd given him a curious look, clearly wondering if his memory was going bad. But Daniel couldn't understand why he hadn't heard from Sadie. His letter should have reached her at least three days before, plenty of time for her to respond. Was she upset with him somehow?

Did she wish he'd told Kevin yes? Was she disappointed that he hadn't taken the opportunity to pay off his father's debt that much faster? But that didn't make sense. He couldn't believe she would approve such a thing. No. His letter must have been delayed, that was all there was to it. She hadn't gotten it when she should have. Her response was likely coming his way right that moment. Tomorrow he'd have a letter. Surely, by tomorrow.

But tomorrow came and went with no word from Sadie. Daniel grew restless, unable to think of anything else. Was something wrong? Was Sadie all right? His mother had written a newsy letter to him and hadn't mentioned anything amiss. But then, why would she be reporting to him about the Sutter family? His mother didn't realize he was courting Sadie.

He wished Abe would write. He'd mentioned Sadie in his last letter, maybe he would do so again. But Abe wasn't likely to write him. The first time had been surprise enough.

"What ails you, boy?" his uncle said when Daniel had jumped up to get his third drink of water that evening. "You fretting about something?"

Daniel put on a smile. "*Nee.* Just thirsty is all."

His aunt looked up from her mending. "Maybe it's time for you to go back to Hollybrook and visit again."

There was nothing he wanted more. But since Kevin had visited, Daniel had been painfully aware of every single cent he spent. And a bus ticket would take over fifty *dollars*. That was fifty dollars to put toward the debt.

"*Jah,* that might be a *gut* idea. Going home to see your family would be much appreciated," his uncle agreed.

Daniel continued to smile even though he knew it had to look glued to his face. "I'll go later. Besides, there's a youth activity this weekend, *Aenti,* and I know you'll want me to go."

His aunt broke out into a wide smile. "Truly? You're wanting to go?"

"I think so. I've met a few people here. I'm sure it will be right fun." He nearly cringed at his own words. Forcing himself to attend the youth function would be anything but fun, but it gave him a reason not to be going home. Besides, he *had* met some people, and they were nice. If he made any effort at all, he could have some good friends there in Render's Bend.

Chloe stood up. "I'm so happy to hear that, Daniel. Truth be told, I've been fretting some about you. Worried that you aren't settling in."

He continued to smile even though his aunt was painfully correct. He wasn't settling in at all, nor did he want to. "I'm fine, *Aenti*," he assured her. "And you have been wonderful *gut* to me. You and *Onkel*."

She flushed with pleasure. "I'm thinking that a hot cup of tea might be nice about now. And some snickerdoodle cookies. How about that?"

Vern laughed. "When aren't your cookies a *gut* idea? Bring in plenty."

Chloe laughed with pleasure. "All right, husband. I'll bring in a plateful."

Daniel pedaled his way to the schoolhouse for the youth function. He'd discovered that it was to be a volleyball game, even though the ground was wet as it had rained even more that morning. In his bicycle basket was a tin of cookies which Chloe had insisted he take. He was happy to, not liking to show up empty-handed at such doings.

When he arrived, he leaned his bicycle against the side of the schoolhouse as the bike rack was already filled to overflowing. He grabbed up the cookie tin and headed for the long table under a newly leafed-out sycamore tree. The table was already sagging under the weight of all the food. Daniel chuckled. He knew that the girls in the district used these opportunities to show off their baking skills. Of course, this would never be admitted as it bordered on pride and vanity—but it was true, just the same.

He immediately recognized Alice, who had approached him at the first youth function he'd attended. He could hardly forget her penetrating blue eyes and the innocence of her smile. He took a deep breath. What must it feel like not to have the weight of your entire family on your shoulders? For he felt the weight of his family so much, that he was surprised he didn't walk with hunched shoulders.

But Alice, there. She looked as if she didn't have a care in the world. He found himself walking toward her with a smile.

"*Gut* afternoon, Alice," he greeted her.

Her eyes lit up. "Why Daniel, how are you? It's nice to see you."

"Likewise." He was standing there grinning until he realized how she could misunderstand his attention. He sobered instantly and looked about frantically, needing a way to escape her happy gaze. "Uh. I'll set these cookies on the table," he uttered, feeling like a fool.

What was the matter with him? He stumbled over to the table and set the tin down beside three other containers overflowing with cookies and dainty slices of cake.

"Hi, Daniel."

Daniel turned to see Howard, a fellow worker at the factory. Daniel was again struck with Howard's sheer huskiness. He appeared huge, until you gave him a second look. Perhaps he seemed so big because of the size of his hands or his thick neck—Daniel didn't know. All he did know was that Howard was a bit overpowering.

"Hi, Howard."

"Glad you could make it. They're about ready to choose sides. You want to be on my team?"

"Sure," Daniel said, glad to be able to talk with someone he knew.

The leader called everyone around in a group and the dividing into teams started. In truth, they had too many people for just two teams, but not really enough for three, so they decided to squeeze everyone onto the make-shift volleyball court at once. There was a lot of laughter and stepping on each other's toes. And more than once, there was a complete crash as two people lunged for the ball at the same time.

Strangely, Daniel found himself having a good time. He laughed right along with the rest of them, causing his share of collisions. Howard was a beast on the court, barging his way to and fro, ramming into anyone foolish enough to get in his way. At first, Daniel thought he was something of a ball hog, but upon watching further, it seemed that Howard was totally unaware of his size or his sheer strength. After a while, the girls would cringe and curl up with their hands over their faces when they saw him coming.

But it was all in good fun, and when they'd played for an hour, everyone dove for the drinks and the goodies. Daniel gulped some lemonade, leaning against the trunk of a tree at the edge of the playground. He gazed around at the crowd, now knowing more than a handful of names. They were nice young people, and he liked them. A part of him felt comfortable amidst them, and that worried him.

Was he beginning to adjust and fit in here? He didn't want to. He didn't want to fit into a place where he'd been forced to come. He didn't want to fit into a place that held no future for him.

But why not? What was the point in stubbornly refusing to

like anything about Render's Bend? Because that was what he'd been doing. He frowned. He'd never been a sour person, but that was who he was becoming, and he didn't like it. The way things stood, he was going to be here for a good long while. Was he planning to be an outsider all that time? Was he planning to dislike every day of his life for the next year or two or even more?

That was no way to live.

God had given him the gift of life and family, and he was squandering both with his selfishness. Thoroughly ashamed of himself, he stood up straight and walked over to the refreshment table. He purposefully started chatting with a group of guys debating about which cake was tastier, offering his opinion with a smile.

When he disagreed with most of them, there was a friendly uproar, and a few of the guys clapped him on the back. Daniel chuckled and stuck with his choice.

Chapter Nine

Sadie tried and tried to calm herself down, but she couldn't do it. She was furious with Aaron. How could he speak to her father like that? How could he agree to continue courting her? Hadn't the two of them agreed that it was over?

By the evening, she was spitting mad. There was nothing she wanted more than to see him and set him straight. Upstairs in her room, she organized and re-organized her drawers, tossing and folding her small amount of clothes over and over. Finally, she stopped, flopping on her bed.

This was ridiculous. Her clothes didn't need straightening. Her side of the room was already painfully clean. She needed to walk off her frustration. She stood and shoved her top drawer closed. Grabbing her shawl from its peg, she flung it around her shoulders and went downstairs. She found her mother in the kitchen, *redding* tomorrow's morning meal.

"I'm going for a walk," she announced, without stopping.

"Wait," Eugenia called.

Sadie stopped and turned to her mother. "What?"

"Are you meeting Aaron?"

Sadie tensed. "I'm just going for a walk, *Mamm*. Is that allowed?" She cringed at her sassy tone, muttering a quick, "Sorry."

"*Jah*, it's allowed, daughter. You're not in a prison cell."

But I am, Sadie thought. *A prison cell, complete with wardens, or whatever they are called.*

"I'll be back soon," she said. She tried to smile at her mother, but she couldn't quite manage it. She turned on her heel and walked out through the washroom and outside. She inhaled deeply of the early spring air. It was crisp and cool and felt good on her lungs. She blinked a few times, adjusting to the falling darkness, and then she started off.

Maybe, she'd walk to Edmund's Pond, but by then, it would be dark, and she wouldn't be able to see anything. Maybe, she should just walk down the road a piece and then come back. That made more sense. But even so, she found herself heading toward Edmund's Pond. When she arrived some time later, it was completely dark.

"This was silly," she muttered to herself. "You can't even walk around the pond in this darkness." She glanced up at the sky. There was a thin cloud covering a nearly full moon. She stood for a moment, debating, and then she headed south toward the Mullet's small farm. She held an unreasonable hope that Aaron would be out and about, and she could tell him exactly what she thought of him.

She marched down the road, careful to stay on the asphalt. She heard a dog barking in the distance, the sound echoing over the empty fields, giving Sadie a feeling of loneliness. Another dog joined him, and the two yipped at each other.

"I guess you two aren't lonely, anyway," she said, smiling softly.

She neared the Mullet farm and was beginning to feel the chill in the air. She shouldn't have walked this far. Her mother was going to worry if she didn't come home soon. She stood on the road, looking up the Mullets' drive.

"Are you there?" she asked aloud. She scanned the property as best she could in the darkness, and then she saw it. A flicker of light coming from the barn. Was it Aaron in there? The chances were good, as it would only be him or his father. Dare she take the risk and peek into the barn? But what if it was Mr. Mullet, and he saw her? How could she explain herself? She couldn't.

Still, it was likely Aaron, and if it was, she could get this load off her chest. She stepped onto the drive, walking slowly and carefully toward the barn. And then she heard whistling. It was Aaron; she could tell. She increased her speed until she got to the barn door. A sudden wave of shyness fell over her, and she wondered at her forwardness. What would Aaron think of her showing up like this? Why, such things simply weren't done. Her foot slipped, and she grabbed onto the side of the barn, making a decided thump.

Well, she'd done it now. She held her breath. Maybe, he hadn't heard her. She turned on her heel, determined to leave before she was discovered. Of all the foolish things she'd done in her life, this topped the list.

"Who's there?" came Aaron's voice from the barn door.

Sadie froze. It was dark; maybe he wouldn't see her.

"Sadie?" His voice was full of incredulity. "Is that you?"

She blew out her breath, her shoulders drooping. She turned to him. "It's me."

"*Ach*, but what are you doing out here?" he cried. "Is everything all right? Is someone hurt?"

She shook her head, wishing he'd point the flashlight somewhere besides her face.

"*Nee*. This was a mistake. Forget you ever saw me." She turned again and started toward the road, but the flashlight had so blinded her that she couldn't see where she was going, and she stumbled.

He was at her side in a flash, taking her arm. "What is it?" he asked. "What's wrong?"

Fine. If he wanted to know, she would tell him.

"Did you talk to my father again?" she asked, her voice now harsh and intent. "About me?"

He swallowed. Even in the darkness and with the light not directed at him, she saw it. Saw his reluctance.

"Come into the barn," he said, guiding her inside the wide double doors.

She allowed him to pull her along into the barn. When they got inside, he set the flashlight on a bench, so it was illuminating them.

"*Jah*, I did."

"How *could* you?" she exploded. "We agreed! This is over!"

"So he told you about it? Your *dat*?"

"*Jah*, he told me. And I was so surprised, I could hardly speak. I thought we'd agreed to end all this. That we'd done enough."

"So did I." He took her arm again, but she shook his loose.

"Aaron, what's going on? Why did you tell my father that you still want to court me? I told him it wouldn't work. That we weren't suited."

He sighed heavily, and she heard the frustration in it. "He asked me if I liked you."

Her chest was heaving, and she was glaring at him. "So you said *nee,* you don't like me."

"There's a problem with that."

"What?" she cried. "What's the problem? We agreed!"

"We've been lying to him, Sadie." He held up his hand. "I know. I know. It was my idea. It seemed pretty harmless in the beginning. But now..." He paused.

"Now what?" she asked impatiently.

"Now I don't want to lie to him anymore. It feels wrong. It *is* wrong."

"It isn't exactly lying, is it? We know we aren't suited because I'm going to marry someone else. In a way, it's the complete truth—if ... if we look at it that way. So, nothing's changed, has it? I don't understand the problem." Even as she spoke, she knew she was stretching things. They had been lying, and she had her conscience to prove it. But she was also trying to make a point, and right then, she was so aggravated with Aaron, she wouldn't have been surprised at anything coming out of her mouth.

He took a step closer and his shadow fell over her face. "Everything has changed. I do like you, Sadie. I couldn't lie about it. I simply couldn't. That would have been a betrayal in my mind. An unforgivable one."

"A betrayal to me? I feel like you did betray me when you agreed to keep courting me. And weren't you upset about the reason my father pursued you in the first place? That had to be insulting."

"About that..." He bit his lip as if trying to decide whether he should reveal something further.

"What?"

"He mentioned it. I was offended and told him so. We discussed it, and there is more to it than me helping him in the fields, Sadie."

She gaped at him. Had her father divulged everything to him?

"He's concerned about you. About your future."

"That's none of *your* business, Aaron," she said, and a sudden dislike for him filled her until she trembled inside.

"It *is* my business," he countered. "Your *dat* made it my business. Look, Sadie. I know you're mad. I know you don't like me at all right now. But I'm in this whether you like it or not. I couldn't lie to your father. I like you. I liked courting you—even if it wasn't real for you."

He stopped and took a breath, his gaze boring into hers. She sucked in a huge breath and shook her head.

"Are you saying you were courting me *for real?* That in your mind, we really were going out together? What about you saying we're just friends spending time with each other? What about that?"

"I know what I said. And maybe I even meant it ... for about five minutes." He chuckled then—a soft, gentle sound that made her even angrier.

"Five minutes! So, you've been serious about me all this time?" Her voice had risen, and she sounded shocked, but with a start, she realized she wasn't as shocked as she sounded. She clamped her mouth shut. Hadn't she known—on some unconscious level—that Aaron did like her, more than liked her? Hadn't she felt the connection between them?

Hadn't Aaron taken up too much space in her *own* mind and thoughts these days?

"*Jah,* Sadie. I've been serious. I knew it was useless as you love Daniel. And you *still* love Daniel. You've made that perfectly clear."

"I ... I do," she murmured, feeling tears burn the backs of her eyes.

"But I think we have to continue with this. Your father won't give you peace unless you do. I'll behave. I'll ignore my true feelings, but I won't lie anymore. I'm courting you for real—knowing it means nothing to you. But I will be honest with your father if he asks. But I won't talk to him about Daniel.

That I won't do. I'll tell him my feelings if he asks. And that's all."

Sadie threw up her hands. "This is ridiculous. How can this possibly work? And for what purpose?"

Aaron shrugged. "It will give you time. And it will give Daniel time. If he comes home with his family's debt taken care of, then your father should be satisfied with him."

Sadie pressed her hand to her mouth. Daniel wouldn't be coming home anytime soon. It would be years, and she knew it. Didn't Aaron realize this? And even if Daniel did somehow manage to come home, she doubted her father would agree to him as her beau. Not after all this.

"So." Aaron brushed his hand over her shoulder, and she involuntarily jumped back. He sighed. "Will you let me take you riding again, Sadie?"

She shook her head. "How can I, Aaron? You just said you didn't want to lie to my father anymore. But I'll still be lying."

"Not if you tell him the truth."

"What do you mean?"

"Tell him that you don't want to go riding with me but that you will."

Her forehead furrowed. "How will that help anything?"

"It will show him that you want to obey him. There is that."

"I *don't* want to obey him."

A flash of pain shone in his eyes for a brief second before he said, "I know that, too. But I also know you, and if you continue to ignore him, it will haunt you."

Her eyes filled with tears then. It was true. It would haunt her. How could Aaron know her so well? Annoyed with him even further now, she swiped the tears from her eyes.

"Fine," she snapped. "I'll go riding with you, but I'll tell *Dat* that I don't want to go."

He grinned then as if hugely relieved. "I'll come get you tomorrow evening at seven-thirty. Will that suit?"

No, it wouldn't suit, but then, when did her opinion matter in this case? "Fine," she said again.

She turned to go, and she was almost sure she heard Aaron mumble, "I'm sorry, Sadie," as she left the barn.

But she didn't leave alone. He was right beside her. She gave him a sharp look.

"I'm not letting you walk home alone in the dark," was all he said.

Chapter Ten

Sadie lay in bed that night wondering what in the world had happened? How had she found herself in this position again? She'd had a plan ... a good one, or so she thought. Cut it off with Aaron. Get a job. Pay for help.

But that had turned upside down. Every bit of it.

Maybe, she'd still get a job. Maybe she'd use her money to run away to Render's Bend. She nearly snorted out loud. She and Daniel would be able to live off her money for how long? A month? Two? And would they be married by an *Englisch* judge? Because they certainly couldn't be married in the church. Not the way things stood.

She was grasping at straws.

Aaron was coming the following evening at seven-thirty. *Ach,* but what would they even talk about? At that point, she was still so angry with him that maybe she wouldn't talk to him at all. She'd just sit there like bark on a tree, fulfilling her father's wishes.

She flipped over in bed.

"What's wrong with you?" Rose muttered from her bed. "You're keeping me awake."

"Sorry," Sadie said, lying still.

"You're flopping about like a baby goat. Is it *Dat* again who's got you all *ferhoodled?*"

"I'm not *ferhoodled.*"

"*Jah*, you are." Rose got out of bed and padded across the floor to Sadie's bed, sitting on the end of it. "What's wrong?"

"You're too young to understand," Sadie said, knowing how cranky she sounded.

"I am not!" Rose cried.

"Shh. *Mamm* will hear you."

"I'm not too young," Rose said sharply under her breath.

Sadie relented. "*Nee.* I s'pose you're not. All right. *Jah*, it's *Dat.* Well, not just *Dat*, but a lot of it is."

"He still going on about Aaron?"

"*Jah.*"

"I'm sorry, Sadie."

"Me, too."

"So, you going to keep seeing him?"

"It seems so," Sadie said with a grudging finality. Then she turned over and closed her eyes, dismissing the conversation and waiting for sleep.

Daniel was getting frantic. Why hadn't Sadie written? He'd never gone this long without an answer from her. Had she forgotten him?

No. That was ridiculous. She wouldn't forget about him. But why hadn't she written? He'd written her again the day before, asking if she'd gotten his other letter. Surely, she'd write back to him now. And if she hadn't gotten his letter, she'd know a letter was missing in the mail somewhere.

Had the topic of his previous letter upset her unduly? He'd told her that he'd turned Kevin down. He'd asked her opinion. There was no cause for her to be upset.

That afternoon, after his shift was over, he left the building determined to continue writing her until he heard back. As he made his way to his aunt's bicycle, he spotted Alice from the youth group standing just outside the wire mesh fence. She looked as if she were waiting for someone. For a split second, he thought she might be waiting for him until reason kicked in. She saw him and waved.

He waved back and then grabbed his bicycle, walking it to the fence gate.

"Hello, Daniel."

"Hello, Alice. You waiting for someone?"

She blushed and nodded. "My brother. Sometimes, I stop by and walk home with him."

He had the sudden thought that maybe that wasn't entirely true—that she *had* come hoping to see him. He grinned with pleasure at the thought. At least, something was pleasant that day.

"That's right nice of you," he commented.

Her blush deepened, and she tilted her head. "My *dat* works here, too. Maybe you know him. Isaiah Wickey? And my brother's name is David."

In his mind, Daniel scanned his fellow workers' faces and names. "*Nee*. I don't think so."

She shrugged. "You're probably in a different area of the factory."

"Probably." He stood there, straddling his bike, trying to think of something further to say.

"Did you enjoy the volleyball game?" she asked.

"*Jah*. I did. It was *gut* fun."

"You've played a lot before. I could tell," she said, and then her eyes widened as she realized that she'd given herself away. So, she had been watching him. His grin widened. This Alice was like a tonic for a person's discouraged spirit.

"*Jah*. Back in Hollybrook, I played." At the mention of his hometown, his thoughts went immediately to Sadie, and he wondered if standing there chatting with Alice was being disloyal.

"That's right. You're from Hollybrook. I reckon you're missing your family."

"I am, at that."

"I can't imagine moving away from my family." Her forehead creased. "Unless there was a mighty *gut* reason for it."

She seemed to be implying something, but he couldn't quite place it. "I did have a *gut* reason."

She nodded slowly. "Folks come up here to work. It's *gut* money." She gave him a wistful look. "I've overheard the talk. Folks come to make money fast, and then, some leave us as quick as they came. Others live here all the time. That would be me." She laughed softly.

"That would be you." He glanced around as if searching for others who lived there full-time. He cleared his throat. "Well, I'll be seeing you around, Alice."

She smiled. "*Jah*. Bye, Daniel."

His name was soft on her lips, and he sensed that she didn't want him to go. *I could stay a minute longer*, he thought, but then stiffened. What was he doing?

"Bye," he said, and he left immediately, peddling down the road as if he were being chased by something.

And he was. His guilty conscience was on his tail, and he pedaled hard trying to leave it behind.

Kevin's mother stood at the door to his bedroom, watching him pack.

"So, you're going then?" she asked, her voice thick with sorrow.

"I'm going. I made a promise."

"Your *dat* is upset."

Kevin sighed and looked over at his mother. He saw her shadowed expression, saw the slight puffiness around her eyes. She'd been crying—not that she would ever admit it, but it was plain to see.

"Everyone knows *Dat* is upset with me." He put on a smile. "What's new? He's always upset with me." His attempt at levity fell flat. He shrugged and went back to stuffing his shirt into his suitcase.

"Not like this," his mother went on. "You could tell that *Englisch* man that you changed your mind."

"I signed a contract, *Mamm*. It's binding."

"You can think of something to get out of it."

Kevin sighed again, wanting more than anything to get out of the house. To get away and not have to witness his mother's pain—pain that he'd inflicted on her.

"I don't want to get out of it, *Mamm*," he told her despite knowing it would hurt her further. "I'm going. It'll be fine. You'll see. And when it's over, I'll have enough money to set myself up."

"Set yourself up doing what exactly?" his mother asked. "Buy a farm? You'll make enough money to buy a farm?"

"A *gut* portion of one, if I wanted to." He walked to her then and took her hand. "I'm not a farmer, *Mamm*. You know that. I've never liked farming."

She swallowed and blinked hard. "Then what? You'll set yourself up doing what?"

"I-I'm not sure yet," he said, and it was true. He had no earthly idea what he was going to do once this adventure was over. He figured something would come to him.

But not farming. Never farming.

"I don't like this," she said, her voice trembling. "You'll be in the fancy world. What's to keep you from..." She stopped herself, her expression stricken.

"I ain't planning on going fancy," he told her gently. "I'm just working with the *Englisch*, not becoming one of them."

"You can't know that," she cried, her voice sharp now. "You'll be rubbing elbows with them all day long. I don't like it. I don't, Kevin. I'm fearful for you."

He took her other hand in his, holding them both in his thin calloused hands. "*Mamm*. Please don't worry. I don't want you to worry. Be happy for me. This is my chance."

"Your chance for what? To leave your home? To leave your family who loves you?" She shook her head. "I don't understand. I've never understood what's inside of you, Kevin. What is driving you so hard? What is it that won't let you rest?"

He felt his eyes burn. He didn't want this. He didn't want some big scene. Not here. Not now. He just wanted to get away. He let go of his mother's hands.

"I need to go, *Mamm*. The bus..."

She stepped back. "I know. The bus is leaving soon. Where are you going anyway? You've told us next to nothing about all this. How do you know it isn't some kind of trick?"

"What kind of trick? What possible reason would Gus Strider have for tricking me? I have nothing." *Not yet, I don't,* he thought. *But soon. Soon, I'll be rich.*

"I don't like this. I have a bad feeling. A real bad feeling."

"*Mamm*, please. Enough. Please. I don't want you to cry, I—"

"I ain't crying," she protested even though he could see her tears. "I'm just worried about my son. It's my right as a *mamm*."

"Fine. Fine. I won't say anymore. But I have to finish packing."

"You going to say *gut*-bye to your father?" she asked pointedly.

"He doesn't want to see me."

"Don't you leave without a *gut*-bye. You'll regret it."

He nodded to pacify her, but he knew he wasn't going to seek out his father before leaving. They'd had further arguments about his decision during the last week, and he was sick of it. And sick of his father. He didn't want to see him again. Not for a long, long time.

"All right," she said, rubbing her hands down the front of her apron. "You'll hug the *kinner*, too."

"*Jah*. I will."

She gave him one last long forlorn look and then turned and left his room. He watched her walk down the hall. Watched the faint sway of her body and the way she always leaned slightly to the left, making her look older than she was. And right then, she leaned more heavily than usual. Because of him. Of course, it was because of him.

Nothing he did ever pleased his parents. It was useless to try.

You haven't tried, he chided himself crossly. *You have never really tried to please them.*

Shoving his self-recriminations aside, he turned back to his suitcase.

Chapter Eleven

Sadie was beside herself. She had decided she couldn't continue writing Daniel, but now she realized just how cruel she was being. It wasn't her intention, of course, but Daniel wasn't to know that. He was likely waiting for her response. And not getting it, he was likely worrying. She had to get word to him—whether it meant disobeying her father or not.

One more letter. Just one. To let him know she wouldn't be writing him any further.

And how was she going to explain that? Was she breaking up with him? Was it over? Her heart lurched. No. It couldn't be over. She loved Daniel.

She pulled at the neck of her dress, trying to loosen it from her throat. She had the strangest sensation of choking. But the neck of her dress wasn't tight—it wasn't pressing against her throat at all. She swallowed, still feeling the pressure.

She needed to write to Daniel. She could have her friend Muriel send the letter. That way Sadie could tell her father honestly that she hadn't sent any further letters to Daniel.

Liar, she thought and flinched.

But she couldn't bear the thought of Daniel wondering and worrying what had happened to her because she wasn't answering his letters. Each letter she'd received that week from him was more frantic than the last. Thankfully, Rose had fetched the mail every time and her father didn't know Sadie had received them.

But none of that helped Daniel.

She sat now on the edge of her bed with her notebook in her hand.

Dear Daniel,

I have gotten your letters. I'm sorry. I can't always write...

She paused. What reason could she give? She swallowed—she couldn't give a reason. She couldn't bear to tell him how her father felt about him.

· · ·

I'm so sorry. I know you've been worried. I'm glad you turned Kevin down. What he's going to do sounds reckless and dangerous. Imagine spending all that time with the Englisch, *doing whatever they want him to do. Imagine having cameras on him all the time. It doesn't bear thinking about.*

I hope things are going well with you. I pray that you're happy in Render's Bend.

Love,

Sadie

It was an awful letter, and she knew it. It said nothing really, only her disapproval of Kevin's plan. But at least, Daniel would receive something. Dare she write more? Tell him the truth of things?

But how could she tell him that she was riding out with Aaron? How could she tell him her father had chosen Aaron to be her beau?

Telling him something like that when he was miles and miles away and couldn't do anything about it, would be cruel. She just couldn't do it to him. He had enough to worry about without adding this to his burdens.

Without thinking about it another minute, she stuck the letter into an envelope and hurried downstairs.

"*Mamm*, I'm going to Muriel's house for a bit," she said before slipping out the side door and heading for the barn to fetch the bicycle. It was plenty warm enough to bike that day, and it would be considerably faster than hitching up the pony cart.

In truth, Sadie was a bit embarrassed to ask Muriel to post the letter for her. She hadn't spent much time with Muriel for quite a while. She saw her at church and at youth functions, but she hadn't made any effort to go over and visit with her. But then, neither had Muriel come to see her. Still, it wasn't very friendly.

When she reached Muriel's house, she saw her friend out back with the chickens.

"Muriel," she called.

Muriel paused and looked toward her, breaking out in a smile. "*Ach*, is it you, Sadie? Goodness, you haven't come by for an age."

Sadie jumped off the bike and leaned it against the barn. "I know. I'm sorry. And you're going to think me terrible—"

"Why would I do that?" Muriel interrupted her, laughing. "I haven't been by to see you, either."

Sadie pulled the envelope from her waistband. "Will you mail this for me?"

Muriel's brow rose. "Who is it to?" But then she saw the address. "Daniel Jantzi. So. I was right all along. You and

Daniel are sweet on each other. *Ach*, but you must be missing him."

Sadie swallowed. "I am. Can you mail this for me?"

"Why can't you mail it for yourself?"

"It's just... Well, my *dat*..." Sadie blew out her breath and once she'd glanced around to assure herself that they were alone, proceeded to tell Muriel the whole story. Muriel's eyes got bigger and bigger the longer Sadie went on. When she was finished, Muriel shook her head.

"But fathers don't do that here. Isn't that more like the olden days in Europe or something?"

Sadie shrugged. "I don't know. But my *dat* insists that he's doing this for my own *gut*."

"I never heard of such a thing. And you have to obey him?"

Sadie stared at her friend.

Muriel grimaced. "I see what you mean." She took the letter. "I'll mail it for you."

"Thank you."

Muriel hesitated. "What's Aaron like?"

"What?"

"He's so quiet. I've often wondered what he's like. He hasn't really opened up to the community as far as I can tell. He keeps to himself. What's he like?"

"He's nice." *At least usually,* Sadie thought. At the moment, she wasn't any too pleased with him. In truth, she wasn't any too pleased with anyone at that moment—including herself.

"Just nice? Is that all you can say?"

"All right. He can be funny sometimes. And he's asked my opinion on things. Once, he let me drive the buggy."

"He let you drive, and he just rode along?" The surprise was evident in her tone.

"*Jah*. It was strange, but I liked it."

Muriel shook her head as if she couldn't believe it. "No guy I know would do that."

"Well, he did."

"What else?"

Sadie saw the eagerness in her eyes. What was this? Was Muriel interested in Aaron? Her brow tightened, and she found herself not pleased.

"There is nothing else," she said.

"I think he's handsome. It can't be that bad spending time with him."

"I didn't say it was bad. It's just forced, and it's Daniel I like."

Muriel studied her for a long moment. "You like Aaron, too."

"I do not!"

"I know we haven't spent much time together lately, but I know you, Sadie. And you like Aaron, too. I can see it on your face."

"I do not, Muriel."

Muriel shrugged. "Fine. Deny it."

Sadie bit her lip to keep from saying more. Muriel was doing her a huge favor by posting her letter, and she needed to bear that in mind.

"Sadie?"

"What?"

"I'm sorry you're having such troubles lately, and I'm sorry Daniel had to go to Bender's Corner. How long will he be gone?"

"Forever, I think," Sadie said, shaking her head.

"Must seem that way. I've heard it's bad for the Jantzis right now."

"It is bad."

"Seems to me like the father should be the one to go north. Or the whole family or something. Don't seem quite right to put it all on Daniel."

"I know, but Daniel was willing."

"Which is admirable. Your *dat* should be happy with him."

"That's what I think."

"Want to come inside for a while?" Muriel asked.

"I better not. Thank you so much for mailing the letter for me, Muriel. I'll see you at preaching Sunday, though, all right?"

"*Jah.* See you then." Muriel squeezed Sadie's hand, and Sadie turned and left.

Chapter Twelve

Daniel read Sadie's letter. Far from feeling better for having heard from her, he felt worse. Her letter didn't seem right. It was strained. And what had she meant by saying she couldn't always write. Why not?

He knew asking her by mail wouldn't satisfy him. He needed to see her, needed to look into her eyes and read what was there.

He couldn't spare the money, but he was going to have to go home. And the sooner, the better. He was going to get to the bottom of this. He had to. He felt Sadie slipping from his fingers, and it sent a shock waves through him.

He had a hard time believing that she would give up on him so easily, but something had changed. Something in her was different. His mind latched onto the image of Aaron Mullet. Did Aaron have anything to do with this? Daniel had dismissed his fears about Aaron after seeing Sadie the last time, but now, he wasn't so sure. Perhaps he was hasty in shelving his concerns. Perhaps there was something going on between Sadie and Aaron, after all. He wished he could come right out and ask someone. His brother, maybe.

But no. He needed to ask Sadie. It was only right. He should have asked her the last time he was there. If only he hadn't chickened out—because that was what it had been. He'd been scared to hear her answer. And now here he was, torturing himself with the questions he hadn't asked.

For Sadie, the days blurred together with a painful sort of monotony. She had resigned herself to simply being an obedient daughter. She comforted herself knowing that at least Daniel had received a letter from her, for Muriel told her that she'd mailed it that same day Sadie had given it to her. So, there was that.

She didn't allow herself to be excited or even interested in Aaron coming around. In truth, she wasn't angry at him anymore. He was being manipulated the same way she was, except that he didn't seem to mind. But on principal alone, she couldn't allow herself to enjoy their time together. Lately, though, it was becoming more troublesome. She had to bite back her laughter, and she had to force maintaining her sullen moods because Aaron did make her laugh. Even when there was nothing funny in her life, he was entertaining. But, she had to pretend he wasn't. Not only in front of him, but when she was alone. When a smile would begin to form on her face, she forced it away.

She *had* to. She couldn't let herself like him. She was already being unfaithful to Daniel. She couldn't make it worse by enjoying it.

Aaron liked her. Even if he hadn't already told her, she would know it. He was animated when they rode out together, and he was always happy to make another date to take her out in his buggy. He never commented on her sour moods. He never tried to force her to smile. It was like he was biding his time, enjoying himself whether she did or not.

It was aggravating. Was there no end to his good moods?

"Sadie?" he asked her now as they headed back to her house.

"*Jah?*"

"I'm thinking about going back to Wisconsin."

Now that got her attention. She stiffened. "What?"

"*Jah.* To see my brothers."

She let out her breath. "Oh. You mean to visit them."

He studied her face. "What did you think I meant?"

"I..." She shook her head. "Nothing."

"You mean to live? You thought I meant to live there again?"

She didn't answer him.

"I heard your relief when I told you otherwise," he said quietly.

"*Nee*, you didn't," she huffed out.

"*Jah*, I did." He was grinning now, looking mighty pleased with himself.

"This is close enough to my house," she snapped. "Let me out here." *Ach,* but what was wrong with her? He was right. She had been upset thinking he was moving—if only for that brief moment.

"I'll take you to your drive," he said. But then he started whistling, and it was all too much.

"Will you stop it?" she cried. "I can't stand it another minute."

He pulled up on the reins. "You can't stand what?"

"I can't stand the way you're always so chipper. The way you always make jokes when we're together. The way you're always in a *gut* mood when you see me." Her eyes burned with anger. "And now, you're whistling! It's... it's too much!"

He gazed at her, not looking in the least upset. "Sadie, you can be as angry with me as you like."

"I *am* angry," she blurted.

"It's all right. I don't mind."

"Why don't you?" she asked, frustration filling her. "What's wrong with you, anyway? I've been awful to you, and you just keep coming back."

He smiled at her and even in the shadows, she could see the tenderness in his eyes. "Of course, I keep coming back. And I'll continue to come back. You like me, Sadie, I know you do. You're upset, and I don't blame you. Truly, I don't. But I think your *dat* is right—"

"*What?*" she shrilled. "You think he's right to force me to go out with you? You think he's right to take away my right to choose—"

He placed his fingers in her lips, silencing her. He leaned closer. "Let me finish," he said gently. "I think your *dat* is right that we belong together. I don't think he is right to force it. I don't think he is right not to listen to you. But Sadie, I love you. I have from the first time we were together."

She gasped, feeling his touch sear through her lips. He *loved her?* No. *No.* This was completely out of hand.

"You ... you *can't*," she whispered through his fingers.

He took his hand away and leaned even closer. He brushed his lips against her cheek and whispered back, "It's too late, Sadie."

She stared at him wide-eyed, while she fumbled at her side, searching for the handle on the door. When she found it, she yanked the door open, almost tumbling out onto the road. And then, without a further word, she started running. Her drive was just ahead, and she raced to it. She ran blindly toward the side door of her house, ignoring the tears that fell down her face. When she burst inside and slammed the door shut, she sank against the wood until she was squatting on the floor.

No. No. No. He couldn't love her. He *couldn't*. Only Daniel loved her. Only Daniel.

Ach, Aaron, why? Why did you have to tell me? The tears continued down her face until she realized she could be discovered, all hunched up there, crying. She sniffed and wiped at her cheeks. Then she stood and squared her shoulders. She sniffed again and marched through the kitchen, grateful no one was there. Nor did she see anyone as she trod up the stairs to her room. She fell inside her doorway and there was Rose, gawking at her.

"Don't ask," Sadie managed to croak out. And then she collapsed on her bed without changing into her nightgown. She pulled at the quilt, loosening it under herself and then dragging it over herself.

Dear Lord, but this was a mess.

And worse, oh so much, *much* worse was the burning truth that she didn't want to face.

Because she was *glad*. Glad that Aaron loved her.

Choking back a sob, she buried her face in her pillow.

Chapter Thirteen

Daniel could hardly sit still on the long bus ride to Hollybrook. *I'm coming, Sadie,* he repeated over and over inside his head. He was trying to work out how he was going to see her without walking right up to her house and knocking on the door. The problem was, he didn't have much time. He could only stay in Hollybrook that night or he wouldn't make it back to work on time for his Monday morning shift. He didn't have time to leave a letter in her mailbox suggesting a meeting time.

Because what if she didn't see it in time? What if he squandered the only night he had there in town?

He was going to have to go directly to her house—oh, not to the door. No. He'd linger at the end of her drive. Surely someone would show up, and he could get a message to her. Or ideally, she'd come out of the house and see him.

No one knew they were courting, but at that point, he didn't care much who found out as long as he could see her. He grimaced. Except Aaron. He hoped that Aaron wouldn't show up. Daniel certainly didn't want him to figure out his desperation to see Sadie.

His mind whirled over the possibilities, creating terrible scenarios. What if Aaron was there to pick up Sadie? What if the two of them were planning an evening together, and Daniel was just standing there on the road staring at them? What if Sadie was hurrying to meet Aaron instead of him.

Ach, but he needed to get his mind under control. This kind of thinking did no good at all.

When the bus finally arrived in Hollybrook, Daniel got off with a heavy feeling of foreboding. He'd done quite a job of depressing himself during the journey. He needed to shake it off. He glanced around the parking lot, wondering how he was going to get to Sadie's place. He could walk, but he hated to take the time.

Just then, he saw a buggy approach, and he recognized Ebenezer Yoder driving. Eb slowed his buggy down before stopping beside the bus.

"Is that you, Daniel?" the old man asked with a grin.

"It is. How are you doing, Eb?" Daniel greeted him.

"Doing right fine. Just picking up a package from the bus. The wife's cousin sent her some special quilt pieces. What makes them so special, I ain't got a clue. But I'm here to fetch them just the same. You need a ride?"

"I do. Can you drop me at Lander Road?"

"I can. But that ain't where you live, son." The old man chuckled.

"I know. I have a few errands to run before going home."

"I can wait while you do your business and take you right to your doorstep."

"I appreciate it, but it ain't necessary. A ride to Lander Road would be a big help, though."

"Whatever suits," Ebenezer said. He went over to the bus driver who was unloading people's luggage from the compartment beneath the bus. Ebenezer grabbed a medium-sized box and came back to the buggy. He put it in the back and both men got in.

Ebenezer regaled Daniel with all the antics of the new milk cow he'd purchased at auction the month before. Daniel's mood lifted as Ebenezer went on and on about it. By the time they reached the intersection of Lander Road, Daniel was chuckling heartily.

"Thank you for the ride," he said.

"My pleasure," said Ebenezer. "You tell your folks hello for me, would you?"

"I will." Daniel grabbed his small bag and got out, waving the man off. Then he turned east on Lander Road toward the Sutter property. Some of his earlier nervousness was back, but he ignored it, focusing his mind on the image of Sadie's face.

When he got to her farm, he set his bag under a maple tree at the side of the road. Then he leaned against the trunk and prepared to wait. He saw one of their barn cats slinking around the side of the barn, and he saw a couple goats in their outside pen, putting their knobby front legs on the fence, bleating. But there was no sign of anyone. How long would he have to wait?

He was prepared to wait the rest of the day if that was what it took, but surely not. Sooner or later, someone would leave the house to tend to some chore or other. He only hoped it wasn't Sadie's folks. He hoped it was either Sadie herself or Rose. In truth, he wouldn't mind the other sisters, either, but they'd likely tell their parents he was there. Rose wouldn't. She'd already proved her trustworthiness.

He sighed and sent up a prayer, and not two minutes later, he heard the side door bang shut. He straightened and peered through the low branches.

Sadie!

His breath caught. *Oh, dearest Gott, thank you for answering my prayer.*

He took off toward the barn, keeping as far back as possible so as not to be seen from the house. She was heading into the barn and hadn't seen him yet. The barn cat meowed loudly when Daniel joined him around back of the barn. And the silly thing kept meowing. What was wrong with it? Was it a guard cat or something? Daniel had never heard such a ruckus.

The barn door was sliding—whether open or shut, he couldn't tell. And then, there she was circling the barn.

"*Ach*, Teddy, what are you cry—" Sadie looked up at Daniel and froze. Her eyes widened and he could see she was sucking in her breath.

And then she exploded toward him, throwing herself in his arms.

"Daniel!" she cried. "Is it you? When did you get here? How did you get here?"

He laughed and held on tightly. "The bus," he murmured into her *kapp*. "*Ach*, Sadie, it's *gut* to see you."

They stood there, smashed together in embrace. Daniel's relief was so overpowering that he wanted to sob. Instead, he just kept repeating Sadie's name over and over. Finally, she pulled away, looking up at him.

"I didn't think you were coming," she said, her eyes filled with tears.

"I had to see you." His throat tightened. Now that he was there, he didn't want to ask her about Aaron, but he knew he must.

"I'm glad." She smiled. "I've missed you."

But then, she looked away. Only for a mere second, but he saw it. There was something wrong. He could sense it now. Something was troubling her.

"Sadie?"

She blinked. "*Jah?*"

"Is everything all right?"

Again, the fleeting glance away and then back. She smiled. "Everything is fine now. You're here."

"Only until tomorrow."

Her expression fell. "Tomorrow?"

"I have to take the bus back tomorrow. I have to work on Monday."

She nodded. "*Jah.* Of course, you do." Her smile widened, but he could see that she was forcing it. "But you're here now, and that's wonderful *gut*."

"Wonderful *gut*," he repeated, unable to ignore the warning lights flashing in his head.

She took his hand and together, they leaned their backs against the barn, looking out over the freshly tilled fields.

"Did you get my letter?" she asked softly.

"I did." He looked down at her. "You said... Well, you said you weren't always able to write. What did you mean?"

A look of panic flashed in her eyes, and his stomach tensed. What was going on? There was something she wasn't telling him.

"Is it Aaron?" he blurted.

Her mouth dropped open. "A-Aaron? What do you mean?"

"Is he the reason you can't write? Because you're with him now?" His words raced out, and he could see the impact they were having on her. She flinched with each one. It had to be true. It had to be, or she would never react like this.

He dropped her hand. His face hardened—he could feel it. He narrowed his eyes, searching her face.

"It's—it's not what you think," she stammered. "Truly, it isn't."

"How do you know what I'm thinking?" he asked and cringed at the harshness of his tone.

"I can see it in your eyes," she said, more quickly now. "It's not like that."

He faced her squarely. "Then you tell me how it is."

Her forehead creased. "How did you even know... I mean, how come you asked me about Aaron?"

"Because my brother saw you with him, that's why."

"Abe? Abe saw me?"

So she knew which brother he was talking about without even asking. She had to have known that Abe saw her.

"*Jah*. Abe."

"But that was a long time ago. He just now told you?"

Daniel let out his breath. "*Nee*. He told me right afterward."

A look of confusion swept over her face. "But you and I have seen each other since then, and you're just now asking?"

He swallowed. "Does that matter? Tell me what's going on, Sadie."

She shook her head and now looked afraid. But why in the world was she afraid? Did she think he would hurt her if he knew the truth? He drew in a breath. "Just tell me the truth, Sadie," he said in a near whisper. "Is Aaron Mullet courting you? Are you riding out with him?"

Tears filled her eyes and trickled down her cheeks. "It ain't what you think..."

"You either are or aren't," he said, impatient now. "Tell me what's going on."

She squeezed her eyes closed, and it was all he could do to resist taking her in his arms. He wanted to hold her, comfort her, kiss away her tears, but how could he? She was betraying him. He should feel only anger toward her, but it wasn't just anger he felt. It was hurt and confusion and frustration.

And helplessness.

She sucked in a breath, and he heard it shake through her. "It's my *dat*," she finally said.

"Your *dat?* What does he have to do with this?"

"He's... He's decided that I should marry Aaron."

Daniel jolted back. *"What?"*

She looked at him through her tears. "You heard me."

"That makes no earthly sense."

"I know," she said, and her voice caught. "But that's the truth of it. He thinks Aaron is the right match for me."

He shook his head. "I don't understand."

She swallowed. "He asked Aaron to court me."

Daniel couldn't believe what he was hearing. He stared at her, stupefied. "What?" he asked again.

"And Aaron agreed."

"What?"

"Please don't keep saying that," she said, muffling a sob. "This is hard enough to tell you."

"Did you tell your father we were courting?"

She nodded, looking miserable. He stared at her until the truth of it dawned on him.

"He... He doesn't want me courting ... you." The words jerked from his lips.

She grabbed his arm. "It's not you, Daniel. Truly, it isn't. But you're going to be up north for a long time— You're not going to be here..."

He shook her hand off and stepped back again. "So this is all about my family's debt? Your *dat* doesn't want us courting because of my father's debt?"

He'd never seen such a dejected look on anyone's face as the one that covered Sadie's face right then. His heart squeezed painfully, and he had to catch his breath. How could this be? How?

"So if I wasn't working to help my family, then it would be all right? You and me? We'd be all right in his eyes?" His words were acid—he was so choked with resentment he could barely see straight. Resentment toward his father and Sadie's father and maybe even the whole world filled him, twisting through his entire being.

She didn't answer; she only stared at him, her eyes round and moist with tears.

"I need to come back to Hollybrook," he said, desperate now. "I need to come back quickly and forever."

"But how?" she asked. "What you're doing... What you're doing is noble, Daniel. And worthy."

"Not if I lose you," he said.

She pressed her hand to her mouth. There was something more. He could see it. He stared at her, hoping she would tell him what it was, but she said nothing. And then she looked away and sighed.

"Is there more?" he asked.

Chapter Fourteen

Sadie couldn't meet his eyes. What more could she possibly tell him? He was angry, and she didn't blame him. But there was nothing for it. He was going back to Render's Bend, and she was staying here. He would be up to his neck in paying down his father's debt for years.

And she was staying here.

Ask me, she pleaded silently. *Ask me to marry you. Ask me to run away with you. Ask me to defy my father and come with you...*

But he didn't. He rubbed his hand over his forehead, and she could feel the anger emanating from him.

"Daniel?" she whispered.

His gaze jerked to her. "What? What do you want me to say?"

She flinched and shook her head. "I don't know."

"I'm going to figure this out. I'll be back. Much sooner than anyone thinks. Much sooner." There was an odd look on his face then, as if he'd decided something terrible.

"You're going to walk away from the debt then?" she asked, half hoping and half dreading. What kind of a person would that make him?

"*Nee*," he said, giving her an unbelieving look. "How could I do that? This is my family... my father."

And I'm your girlfriend—your almost fiancée.

"I have a father, too," she murmured.

"What's that supposed to mean?" he snapped.

"I have an obligation to my father, too."

"So, you want to marry Aaron? Is that it?"

She blanched. Anger zipped through her. "You won't abandon your father, but you're mad because I won't abandon mine?" She braced herself, waiting for his answer.

"That isn't the same," he cried. "That isn't the same thing at all!"

Her face crumpled, and she fought her tears. But it was the same thing. Couldn't he see that?

He groaned and stepped closer again. "Sadie, I didn't come

here to fight. I didn't. I came because I was worried. I... I'm so sorry. Truly. About all of this. But I'll work it out. I promise."

"How?"

He blinked rapidly. "I have a plan. I'll be back within a year. I will. I'll join the church, and we'll be married."

She pressed her hands against her chest, wondering how that could possibly happen. But if he said it would...

He swallowed and took her hands in his. "Don't let your father force you into anything. He wouldn't get the backing, you know. The bishop wouldn't agree to what he's doing. Neither would the elders. It ain't right what he's doing."

She squirmed. She already knew that, but hearing it as criticism from Daniel's lips was upsetting no matter how true it was. Something in her rose up to defend her father, but she quickly pressed it down.

She bit her bottom lip, her mind whirling and confusion edging closer.

"Yet you will stay true to *your* father..." she murmured.

"Sadie, it ain't the same." He was pleading now. "And I'll be back. So fast that everyone will be surprised."

She blinked as tears fell down her face. "If you say so, Daniel."

"I do say so. I do." He smiled at her then. "It'll be all right.

You'll see."

It'll be all right.

How many times had she told herself that? How many times had she heard it?

But it wasn't always true. Would it be true this time? She wasn't sure. But everything *would* all right—it *had* to be all right. Just maybe not in the way she hoped. And now, as she stood in front of Daniel, she wasn't even sure what she hoped anymore. She wished she could travel back in time. She wished Daniel had already joined church, and they were already married.

Then this would have played out so much differently.

But wishing for the past or wishing things weren't as they were, did nobody any good. She had to take life the way it was and make something from it. Something good and lovely and worthy.

Could she? Could she take this mess and make something good out of it?

"Sadie, I'll be back."

She nodded and forced herself to smile. She didn't feel it much right then, but she would gather her courage as the days went on. She would trust God. And it *would* be all right. One way or the other.

"Thank you for coming to see me, Daniel. I'm sorry we

argued." And she was.

He grinned at her then, and she saw his usual good nature returning. "I had to come see my girl, didn't I?"

She smiled, then. A real smile. "You did… Daniel? How are you going to do it? How will you come home sooner?" The only thing she could think of him doing was the one thing she didn't want him to do. She was afraid to mention it, afraid to ask him if he was going to work for the television producer. She didn't want to hear his answer. Didn't want him to disappoint her and fill her with doubt as to who he really was.

"I have a plan," he said. "Trust me, Sadie."

He leaned close and looked deeply into her eyes before touching his lips to hers. She trembled at his touch and slowly moved her lips beneath his, kissing him back.

She pulled away slightly. "Hurry back," she whispered, praying his idea would work and that it was a good one.

"That is exactly what I plan to do," he said before pressing his mouth to hers once again.

A half an hour later when Daniel left her standing behind the barn, Sadie was still for a good long while. She touched her fingers to her mouth, savoring Daniel's kiss. Any minute, her mother would be calling her, wondering what was taking her so long. But Sadie needed this time. She needed to close her eyes and breathe and muster up her trust in God. Because wasn't that what it all came down to? Trusting God?

"I do trust you, dear Lord," she whispered between her fingers. "I do trust you."

And she had to trust Daniel, too. Wasn't that part of loving someone? Trusting them? She let out her breath and leaned against the barn siding. She could feel the roughness of the boards through her dress. She heard their milk cow lowing to her right. The chickens clucked as she watched them pecking about, stirring up the dust in their pen.

She nodded ever so slightly, deciding that it truly *was* going to be all right. She would trust God and trust Daniel and even trust her father. She certainly didn't have all the answers. Not even by half. But it was all right. She had committed herself to a life of faith, and wasn't this part of faith? Believing, when so many of the answers were hidden?

What was she going to do about her father's insistence that she marry Aaron? She was going to try again. Try to talk to him, try to share her heart. She feared he wouldn't listen—for what had changed? But maybe she had. Maybe she was stronger now. Maybe he would at least listen and give her some time, and then Daniel would be back, and her father could see him in a different light.

And Aaron? What about him? She raised her chin. She'd made herself clear with Aaron—he knew she was in love with

Daniel; that she planned to marry Daniel. What more could she do than be honest?

Be honest with yourself, Sadie, came the unwelcome reply. She gave a soft snort. She was expecting too much of herself on that front. How could she expect not to feel anything toward someone else just because she was in love with Daniel? She was human, wasn't she? And knowing that Aaron was nice and enjoying his company didn't have to mean a thing.

Daniel, hurry back. Hurry back so things will truly be all right again.

But for now, she had to live with the uncertainty. She knew that. Which—of course—was also part of having faith. What was that verse she liked so well? It was in Hebrews; she remembered that. Something like—*faith is the assurance of things hoped for, the conviction of things not seen...*

Yes, that was it. She would live true to that verse and have faith in the future, even though things didn't look all that possible right then.

She squared her shoulders and made her way back around the barn. Just then, she heard her mother calling her.

"Sadie? Where did you get to? I need you in here."

"Coming, *Mamm,*" she hollered back as she walked across the lawn.

The End

Continue Reading...

Thank you for reading **Sadie's Absent Beau.** Have you read **Sadie's Story #1, The Factory Worker**? If not, you can find it **HERE:** http://ticahousepublishing.com/amish.html

COMING SOON is **Sadie's Story #3**, the final book of Sadie's Story. In the meantime, **are you wondering what to read next?** Why not read **Hollybrook Valentine?** **Here's a peek for you:**

Lily Umble tucked her feet beneath her dress and leaned her back against the bale of hay. Being late January in Indiana, it was cold up in the barn loft though she was well-bundled—even wearing two scarves around her neck. Her fingers were slightly cramped around her pencil, but in truth, she didn't mind.

This was her secret place. Not really secret, of course, but no one in her family would venture up into the loft this time of year, unless it was to fork down more hay. And she never climbed up there without making sure there was plenty of hay in the stalls already. She wasn't about to risk getting caught up there—especially by her father.

Love, like the night owl, soars the sky

Searching ... searching for a place to land,

To roost, hidden among the branches.

Pure love growing stronger with each interloping circle

wings strengthening—

Something sounded, and Lily froze. Had someone come into the barn? She didn't dare move to the edge of the loft to look; she'd give herself away for sure. Her pencil hovered motionless over her tablet of paper. She didn't breathe.

It was footsteps—she heard them distinctly now. Someone below cleared his throat, and she sucked in a shallow breath. She recognized the sound. Thank goodness, it wasn't her father; it was her brother. Still, she didn't want Samuel knowing she was up there, either. Obedient to a fault, he would immediately rat her out to their father.

"Hey there, Blondie," she heard him coo to their new jersey cow. "I'm just checking on you. You're a *gut* girl, you are..."

Lily heard him slap the cow's flank.

Go away, Samuel. Go away, go away.

Samuel continued to talk to Blondie, but Lily couldn't make out what he said after his first few words. She remained still, not daring to move a muscle. If she shifted even the slightest bit, pieces of hay could flitter down from the loft and she would give herself away.

"Hey, Samuel," said their younger sister Miriam, coming through the barn door with clomping footsteps. "Where's Lily?"

VISIT HERE To Read More:

http://ticahousepublishing.com/amish.html

Thank you for Reading

If you **love Amish Romance**, **Visit Here:**

https://amish.subscribemenow.com/

to find out about all **New Hollybrook Amish Romance Releases! We will let you know as soon as they become available!**

If you enjoyed ***Sadie's Absent Beau,*** would you kindly take a couple minutes to leave a positive review on Amazon? It only takes a moment, and positive reviews truly make a difference. I would be so grateful! Thank you!

Turn the page to discover more Amish Romances just for you!

More Amish Romance for You

We love clean, sweet, rich Amish Romances and have a lovely library of Brenda Maxfield titles just for you! (Remember that ALL of Brenda's Amish titles can be downloaded FREE with Kindle Unlimited!)

If you love bargains, you may want to start right here!

VISIT HERE to discover our complete list of box sets!

http://ticahousepublishing.com/bargains-amish-box-sets.html

VISIT HERE to find Brenda's single titles.

http://ticahousepublishing.com/amish.html

You're sure to find many favorites. Enjoy!

About the Author

I am blessed to live in part-time in Indiana, a state I share with many Amish communities, and part-time in Costa Rica. One of my favorite activities is exploring other cultures. My husband, Paul, and I have two grown children and five precious grandchildren. I love to hole up in our lake cabin and write. You'll also often find me walking the shores by the sea. Happy Reading !

https://ticahousepublishing.com/